Sy

A SCENT OF

JASMINE

Copyright © 1996 by Sylvia Nobel
Kensington Publishing edition: April 1997
Nite Owl Books edition : April 2012

Nite Owl Books
2850 E. Camelback Road, Suite #185
Phoenix, Arizona 85016-4311
(602) 840-0132
FAX (602) 277-9491
e-mail: niteowlbooks@cox.net
www.niteowlbooks.com

ISBN 978-0-9839702-0-0

Cover Design by ATG Productions
Christy A. Moeller – Phoenix, Arizona

Library of Congress Control Number
2003103398

Chapter One

Fierce Arizona sunlight beat down on Andrea Dusseaux as she stood near the curb staring down at the three bulging suitcases which held the sum total of her worldly possessions.

"Smart move, Andie," she admonished herself aloud, wishing she'd asked the cabdriver for help. "Now what?"

A feeling of awe overcame her as she turned to admire the graceful Victorian architecture of the Sundial House Restaurant, the last place on earth she would have imagined Mo to establish roots. The very words "establish" and "roots" seemed a contradiction when thinking of her adventurous friend.

When she tried to move forward, almost stepping out of her left pump, she gasped in surprise. A chunk of melted tar clung to the heel after she extricated it.

"Damn!" she muttered under her breath, and then looked up as a voice from the tree-lined patio called, "Hi. Are you Andrea?"

The sight of the smiling olive-skinned teenager in white

shirt, black slacks and bow tie lightened the feeling of momentary frustration that had knotted her stomach. She answered his smile with one of her own. "That's me."

An easy gait brought him to her side. "I'm Manuel," he volunteered, picking up two of the bags. "Welcome to Sundial House. Maureen's hung up in the kitchen and said for me to take you there."

"Lead the way," she answered, blotting her neck with a handkerchief while wheeling the third suitcase behind her over the bumpy walkway. She hurried ahead of him to hold open the massive wood and stained-glass front door, then followed him inside.

In the narrow, antique-filled foyer, Andrea threaded her way past half a dozen customers waiting beside the highly-polished mahogany staircase, and continued through the dining room where the waiters were putting finishing touches on the white-draped tables. She stepped aside as a young waitress with a tray of bud vases filled with fresh flowers rushed by.

Andrea paused while Manuel backed into one of the swinging doors to allow her entry into the surprisingly modern kitchen—a stark contrast to the old house. As a myriad of delicious smells assailed her, a blast of heat took her breath away. Somewhere in the back, a radio blared.

The wide smile of welcome on Maureen Callaway's familiar round face sent a rush of delight tingling through her.

"Andie! God, am I glad to see you! I'd give you a big hug," she said, wiping her hands on her long white apron, "but I wouldn't want to get anything on that drop-dead suit." The clear hazel eyes appraised her with affection and then fell on the jumble of bags Manuel plumped down beside her.

"What the hell is all this?" Mo inquired, mirth twinkling in her eyes. "I hope they're stuffed full of cash from your divorce settlement."

Andrea gave a wry smile. "I wish." She dropped the

luggage strap and placed her hands on her hips. "What happened to the cool April weather you promised me?"

Mo grimaced. "You had to pick the one freaky hot day to make a liar out of me."

"I'll forgive you after I've had an ice cold shower and changed into ..."

"That's gonna have to wait along with the thousand questions I want to ask you," Mo interrupted, darting a worried look at the clock. "I'm in a real jam today. The lunchtime cook is stuck in Nogales, my hostess called in sick, and you're gonna have to bail me out."

Andrea stared, nonplussed. "Me? How?"

"Robin!" Mo barked to the chubby, dark-haired girl chopping lettuce on the stainless-steel table nearby. "The oven buzzer! Get those rolls out before they burn!" She puffed out a breath as she returned her gaze to Andrea. "You said you wanted hands-on experience in this business, so you'll get hands-on. I've got reservations up the ying-yang, and guess what? You're my hostess today."

Andrea's stomach plunged in panic. "But ... but ..." she stammered. "I don't know what to do! I need some time to ..."

"There *is* no time," her friend moaned, a pleading look entering her eyes. "Grab the stack of menus off the reception desk before the you-know-what hits the fan. Come on, Andie. You can do it! Just pretend you're hosting one of those fancy parties you're so good at."

Madison McKee shifted his weight and leaned back against the sharp corner of the antique buffet to allow two heavy-set women to jostle past him into the dining room. The aroma of food made his stomach rumble, and he fought down another wave of consternation. Twenty minutes had elapsed since the time they should have been seated.

Ordinarily he would not have been so impatient, but it seemed as if the frazzled blonde hostess had seated everyone in the world except him and his waiting party of six other hungry people. He turned to his grim-faced companions and gave an apologetic shrug. Tension tightened his jaw, and once again he fastened his gaze on the hostess. His secretary could have chosen any number of fine downtown restaurants. Why did she have to choose this one?

He approached her for a second time. "Miss," he said, with forced politeness, "I'm sure we had a reservation for twelve-thirty. It's under the law firm of McKee, Pritchard, Skyler and Dunn."

She laid the stack of menus down abruptly. "I'll check again."

"Or," he suggested, stepping close behind her. "It might be under my name, Madison McKee."

Lightly tapping one foot, he watched her scan the reservation book and heard an obvious sigh of irritation when he leaned over her shoulder to read the names. She seemed flustered, and he thought it curious that her hand shook as her slender fingers traced the list.

Suddenly aware of the warm sensual scent of her perfume, he took a step back and let his eyes trail over her. In spite of his agitation, he found himself admiring her impish upturned nose and flawless complexion. Loose strands from her shoulder-length hair clung to her neck.

"Sorry. There's no such reservation. And as you can see," she said, waving an arm toward the lunch crowd, "I don't have a table for seven right now."

Madison glanced into the teeming dining area. "I can see that. But, that is *your* problem. Mine is to make sure my clients are taken care of, and you're making that difficult. We have an important meeting to get back to."

She said nothing, just stiffened and glanced aside, blinking rapidly, her full pink lips compressing into a thin line.

What was the matter with her? It wasn't as if he was

asking for the moon. He was simply asking this woman to do her job. "Look," he sighed, lightly touching her forearm in an attempt to appeal to her sense of reason. "When I asked in the beginning, you said it would be only ten minutes."

"I'm doing the best I can," she said icily, averting her gaze. "I can seat you at two separate tables. Would that do?"

Madison felt his temper rising. "And shout at each other across the room? I think not." Annoyed as he was, his gaze strayed to her full rounded breasts, accentuated by the form-fitting silk blouse.

"What would you like me to do, Sir?" she asked confronting him, with strong emphasis on the 'sir.' "Move someone else?"

Madison drew back in surprise. For the first time, he looked directly into her extraordinary turquoise eyes and saw something there that unnerved him. Inexplicably, he couldn't think of what his next remark was going to be.

Andrea stared at the green flecks gleaming from the depth of his penetrating brown eyes. Who was this arrogant man? *I think not?* she fumed, recalling his sarcastic words. How dare he address her in such a manner? She resisted the urge to slap the insolence from his face. Instead, she forced a wooden smile. "I'll check on the table."

Determined strides bore her into the dining room as she swallowed back angry tears. Although this imperious man didn't look like him, his conduct unleashed the sense of insecurity and helplessness Bernard had so expertly instilled in her for eight years. It made her blood boil to once again experience the feelings of inadequacy and it reminded her of how she'd permitted Bernard's subtle domination to manipulate and stifle her personality.

Ironically, when this stranger walked in earlier, she'd been impressed by his air of self-assurance and noticed, along with every other female in the room, his exceptionally handsome chiseled features. Broad shoulders strained against the material of a beautifully-tailored gray suit. In an absent-minded gesture, he'd combed his fingers through the mass of wavy chestnut hair. She'd even admired the dimples that underscored his smile when he'd first approached her.

But now, his appeal had faded as his demanding manner eclipsed the positive impression she'd formed earlier.

A pony-tailed waitress excitedly ran up to her waving a check. "They're leaving. Give me a minute to put the tables together and you can bring in that gorgeous hunk and his party."

Andrea breathed a sigh of relief. "You're welcome to him," she muttered under her breath.

She paused to compose herself and, with renewed confidence, returned to the front desk, her mood lightened by the prospect of getting rid of this irritating man. She forced a smile. "Your table is ready, Sir."

"Thank you," he said curtly while gesturing to his companions.

You owe me one, Mo, she thought, *for putting me on the spot.* She led the way across the noisy room, her confident steps faltering as she imagined his hostile gaze boring into her.

She handed out menus, noting his companions' satisfied expressions as they drew their chairs up to the well-appointed table by the bay window that overlooked the colorful garden.

"Charming," said one of the men reaching for an olive from the iced relish tray as the exuberant waitress approached them with a basket of hot rolls.

"Good things come to those who wait," she announced eagerly. "Welcome to the best table in the house."

Andrea cringed inwardly at the girl's syrupy enthusiasm, and the way she boldly fastened her eyes on Mr. Obnoxious.

"Thank you, Susan," he said, noticing her name tag.

As Andrea moved away, she heard him quip, "It's so

comforting to see a friendly face." Seething inside, she fled to the mercifully empty foyer and collapsed on the stool, slipping her tired feet out of the high-heeled pumps. She exhaled a deep sigh. Finally everyone had been seated. The antique clock above her head chimed one. Had it only been two hours? It felt as if she'd been in the trenches for days.

In the momentary lull she caught sight of her distorted reflection in the mahogany-framed mirror, noting with a sense of dismay the limp strands of hair dangling around her flushed face. She'd looked a lot more presentable a few hours ago, she thought with a rueful smile. But the long flight from New York, coupled with heat and stress, left her feeling older than her thirty-one years. In addition, she felt irritated that she'd allowed her composure to be shaken by a complete stranger.

She cast a sideways glance into the dining room and studied the man's refined face again. He *was* something— at least to look at, but his conduct toward her was inexcusable.

The jangling of the telephone jarred her from her thoughts and she picked up the receiver. A woman at the other end of the line asked for a table at noon the following day. Andrea flipped the page, running her finger down the sheet. She added the woman's reservation to the list and then her hand froze as she noticed the name directly below it. "Oh, no!" she gasped. The name Madison McKee jumped off the page. *Party of seven, 12:30.*

In a preoccupied voice, she confirmed the woman's reservation and hung up. For several agonizing moments she sat still, one hand pressed to her lips. Why hadn't it occurred to her to look at the next page? Wait a minute! It wasn't *her* fault. For all she knew the big-shot lawyer's secretary could have goofed and made the reservations for the wrong day. But the most likely scenerio was that the hostess had made the mistake.

Suddenly she felt mortified, remembering how rude and confrontational she'd been to the man, embarrassing him in front of his guests. It was bad enough that he had to wait so long for a table. And what if he was one of Mo's regular customers? Regular or not, she knew she had to do something. She slipped her shoes back on and rose from the stool. She'd better tell Mo.

One peek into the hectic atmosphere of the kitchen canceled that thought. There stood Mo amid the clutter of pots and pans, serving spoon in hand, staring at ten or fifteen unfilled lunch orders, mumbling incoherently to herself.

No, Andrea decided, backing away from the door, she'd have to handle this herself. A nice bottle of wine might serve to pacify them. She would reimburse Mo for the expense if the offer didn't meet with her approval.

Gathering courage, she smoothed the wrinkles from her pristine-white linen skirt, fixed a placid smile on her face and marched to his table. The little speech she'd planned died on her lips when she noticed that Susan was already clearing away the lunch dishes. Oops! Too late for wine. Now what?

"Time to tempt you with our spectacular desserts," Susan said in her cloying voice. "They're so luscious, that once you've tried them, you'll never be happy with anything else," she added with a suggestive wink in Madison McKee's direction.

What a little flirt, Andrea bristled, wondering why she should even care about the girl's behavior.

"Excuse me," she interrupted, taking the cue. "We'd be happy to offer you dessert on the house." She ignored Susan's doubletake and met Madison McKee's questioning look. "It appears that the hostess wrote the reservation on the wrong page," she said apologetically, fully expecting to see a gleam of triumph in the man's eyes. Instead she saw a brief look of concern.

"Thank you for offering," he said in a surprisingly courteous tone, "but we haven't time today. Another occasion perhaps?"

Puzzled by the transformation, Andrea nodded politely. "It will be our pleasure, Mr. McKee."

As Madison watched her turn and move gracefully across the room, her shoulders set straight and proud, his gaze involuntarily slid down to her shapely bottom and then back up to the regal tilt of her head.

His feelings of remorse sharpened. *Damn!* He should have realized she was the owner. Justified or not, he'd had no business being rude to her, or to anyone for that matter. Was it the heat, or the fifteen-hour days that were getting to him? Probably both, he thought as he hastily paid the bill, deciding he'd best take a moment to apologize to her for his less-than-gracious behavior.

As he and his party headed for the door, he searched the foyer, but she was nowhere to be seen. Pressed for time, he ushered his companions out to the waiting limousine.

During the short ride back to his office, Madison felt annoyed that his thoughts kept returning to the blonde woman, instead of concentrating on the important meeting ahead. For some reason he couldn't explain, he hated to have her think of him as such a lout. He tried to remember his exact words to her. Had he been *that* difficult? he wondered, remembering the look of anger and defiance reflected in her eyes. No, it had been more than mere annoyance regarding his overbearing manner. There had been something indefinable, almost like a flash of horrified recognition.

A question from one of his companions drew his attention from the puzzle, and by the time they'd entered the building and began the ascent to the twenty-third floor, he'd dismissed the incident from his mind.

The elevator doors gave a soft swoosh as they opened into the walnut-paneled waiting area. Madison waved to

Blanche Kittering, the receptionist, who was on the phone, and motioned to her that he was taking his clients to the conference room. Once there, he seated them at the long, oak table and invited them to study the re-zoning information that his secretary had set out.

He excused himself and crossed the expanse of plush green carpeting to the reception desk. "Any messages, Blanche?"

She turned her attention from the word processor and eyed him over the square reading glasses perched low on the bridge of her nose. "Which stack do you want?"

"The smallest one," he teased, returning her mischievous smile. The buxom woman with the blue-black, beehive and exaggerated false lashes had been a fixture in his father's office even before he'd decided to follow Madison McKee, Sr., into law.

Blanche handed him a few notes and thumbed in the direction of his office. "Your father's in there waiting for you."

He raised a brow in surprise. "What's he doing here? I thought he was lost somewhere on the golf course. My mother said she'd hardly seen him for a week."

She shrugged, palming her hands upward. "Who knows? I think he's having trouble adjusting to retired life. After all, he headed up this place for almost forty years and it's only been two months."

"I guess he's forgotten that's why he brought me up here from the Tucson office."

"Humor him," she said with a wry smile.

Madison nodded, then took four long strides to the door of his office and swung it open. His gaze fastened on the vivid contemporary watercolor that had been delivered that morning. The painting served as a nice contrast to the somber, cherrywood floor-to-ceiling bookcases. The only thing out of place now, he noted with amusement, was his father.

Madison McKee Sr. stood in the middle of the room clad in yellow and brown checked golf slacks and a gold pullover. Hunched over a seven iron, he drew his arms back, then moved them forward, giving a graceful swing upward. His eyes followed the flight of the imaginary ball, then he focused his gaze on Madison. "It's so easy to make a great shot here," he said with a rueful grin. "Why the devil can't I do the same on the course?"

Madison laughed and moved to the well-stocked bar in the corner. He extracted a soda from the refrigerator, popped it open and extended it in his father's direction with a questioning look. McKee, Sr. shook his head.

Madison took a sip and crossed to his desk. "I'd love to visit, Dad, but I've got people waiting in the conference room."

"I know, I know," his father said quickly and then stopped to appraise him. "Hey! You've got six more gray hairs than when I saw you last," he teased. "Slow down. You're only thirty-four for Christ's sake!"

"Look who's talking. Your twenty-three hour days are legendary." He drummed the desk impatiently as he watched his father take another golf swing, obviously stalling. "Okay, Dad, what's up?"

McKee, Sr. stopped and met his son's eyes squarely. "You're not gonna like this, so don't get your dander up till you hear me out. Agreed?"

"I don't think I want to hear it since you put it that way, but okay."

McKee, Sr. planted himself in the chair in front of the massive desk and stretched out his legs. "I need a one-time favor. Russell and I played golf this morning and . . ."

"Damn, you're right. I don't like where this is going."

"You agreed to hear me out," his father said, holding up his hand.

Madison laced his fingers behind his head, and leaned back to stare at the ceiling. "Okay, shoot."

"The deal Russell's got going with these two downtown blocks is in trouble. The law firm he had working on it screwed up and he wants us to take it on."

"Us? Dad!" He banged his fist on the desk. "Russell Stanton and I haven't sat in the same room in four years."

"Things haven't been that good between him and me either since you and Victoria broke up. But we talked about that."

"Oh? Has he finally mellowed?"

"He's willing to let bygones be bygones if you'll do this. He needs the best man for the job and he knows that's you. Here's the situation." He got up and paced back and forth. "The re-zoning application is almost complete and all the lot owners have agreed to sell except one. This stubborn lady's got the two prime pieces he needs."

Madison met his father's gaze. "Tell him to dig a little deeper into his pockets."

"He did that already. Offered her nearly twice what the property's worth and it's still no go."

"Dad, everyone has a price."

"Not this woman. They even threatened to cut off her access to parking on the adjoining lot and she still wouldn't budge. Russell needs the right person to handle this."

"And I'm it?"

"Hey! I didn't send you to Harvard for nothing, and how many men your age do you know are running a firm this size?" he asked, gesturing around the room.

"I'm flattered," he said, recognizing his father's manipulative tactics. "I'll look into it."

"What's there to look into? Be smart here. I don't have to tell you how much money is involved." He leaned in close. "And there's an added bonus. You get a chance to redeem yourself with Russell."

Madison studied the old man's angular face. Four years was a long time for best friends to be estranged, and he'd felt enough guilt over his part in it. "Okay, but I don't care what Russell thinks of me. This is for *you*, Dad."

McKee, Sr. beamed and put out his hand. They shook solemnly and then the older man snatched up the phone and dialed, obviously pleased with himself as he waited.

"Russ? This is McKee," he said, giving Madison a bold wink. "It's settled. You've got your boy!" His eyes gleamed in triumph as he slammed down the receiver.

"Dad, I really have to run. Have them send the files to me." He picked up a pen. "Who's the holdout?"

"The owner of the Sundial House. All you have to do now is charm the pants off Maureen Callaway.

Chapter Two

Thankful that the lunch ordeal was now behind her, Andrea leaned wearily against the wall in Maureen's office and rubbed the blister on her heel.

"My feet will never recover, I'm sure," she said, catching Mo's amused glance from across the room where she lay sprawled on an old plaid sofa, her emerald gauze skirt overflowing onto the floor.

"It's your own fault. You shouldn't try to do hard labor in five-inch heels."

"I could happily choke you for putting me on the spot like that."

Maureen giggled. "Face it, kiddo. Your days of living like Rapunzel in your gilt-edged ivory tower are gone. Welcome to the real world."

"Where do you think I've been for the last year?" Andrea replied, all traces of humor gone from her speech.

"Sorry. I shouldn't have said that." She rolled off the couch, ran to Andrea and flung her arms around her. "It's just that . . . well . . . Why didn't you tell me you were going through such hell?"

Andrea patted Mo's shoulder affectionately. "And what would you have done if I had? Broken into the castle and rescued me? You had your own problems. Christopher was small, you'd just bought this place . . ."

"Oh, Andie. If I could just get my hands on that slick bastard for two minutes . . ."

"He's history. My old life is history. Once I'm through learning the catering business from you, I can go back and kiss that job good-bye too."

"Is selling cosmetics that bad?"

"It's not the cosmetics, it's having to put up with my boss."

"You never told me about that."

"Later," Andrea said, massaging the back of her neck. "I'm hot, I have jet lag and I'm too tired to think right now."

"Let's go home so you can freshen up." She moved to the cluttered desk, leafed through some papers, then stopped and grimaced with pain.

"What's wrong?"

Mo shook her head. "Nothing. Just a headache. It's probably because I've been working so much these last couple of weeks." She yanked open a drawer. "Where the hell is that electric bill?" she grumbled to herself, then slammed the drawer shut and slumped into a sigh. "Thank God Rosie'll be back from vacation tomorrow. I told you about her, didn't I? The retired school teacher I hired last year to manage the restaurant?" Before Andrea could answer, Mo threw her hands up. "Why am I rambling on like this?" She slapped the desk and stood. "We need to get you a shower and a nap. Manuel can help you over to the house with the bags. While you're doing that, I'll run and get Christopher from school."

"I haven't seen that little devil since he was two," she

said, following Mo to the door. "Do you think he'll remember me after three years?"

"Has it been that long?" Mo stopped and laid a hand on Andrea's arm. "Thanks for sending me the plane fare to bring him back to meet you. I sure couldn't have afforded the expense at the time." She shot a glance at her watch. "Whoops! Gotta go."

Andrea grinned and shook her head as Mo bolted out the door. What a character, she thought. Even though they'd come from similar privileged backgrounds, their lives had been vastly different. Her own had been sheltered, while Mo wouldn't have thought twice about hitching a ride with a stranger, or camping out on the beach. But getting pregnant with Christopher seemed to have tamed her, and five years ago she'd veered out of the fast lane and planted deep roots here.

Manuel stuck his head in the door. "Ready to go?"

Andrea nodded and followed him outside into the stifling heat. After arriving at the small white cottage next door, she took one look around the dilapidated interior and concluded that most of the money Mo had inherited from her father had gone into the restaurant.

Later that afternoon, refreshed after a bath and a nap, and dressed in comfortable jeans and a T-shirt, she accompanied Mo back to the restaurant as soon as the babysitter arrived.

"So, how do you like my grand home?" Mo asked as they walked out.

Andrea caught the facetious tone. "It's very . . . um . . . quaint."

"Is that another word for junky?"

"I didn't say that, but it looks like it could use a little TLC."

"I had plans to fix it up, but all the money disappeared into that grand old lady," she said, gesturing to Sundial House. "You have no idea what was involved in renovating it—new plumbing, new wiring, a new roof . . . you name it."

"You've done a great job with it, Mo. And I love that pale yellow trim you added. It looks so perfect with the brick."

"Yeah," she agreed, smiling through a look of dismay. "And just when everything is finally taking shape, I can't enjoy it because those vultures are trying to get their greedy hooks into the place."

Andrea struggled to keep up with Mo, her renewed energy flagging in the oppressive heat. "What are you talking about?"

"Remember that high-powered developer who was trying to buy me out? Well, he still is. He can offer me ten million bucks, but I ain't selling."

"For God's sake, Mo! For ten million you could buy *another* place, a yacht, and maybe have something left over for a handful of tokens for the New York City subway."

Mo fluffed her dark curls in a gesture of impatience. "Let's stop talking about it before I get another headache."

Inside the restaurant, the waiters were setting up the dining room for the evening patrons. Rose linen tablecloths replaced the white, and burgundy napkins pleated into the shape of a fan crowned the long-stemmed wine glasses. Candles flickered on the tables.

Although the kitchen activity was at its peak, the dinner crew appeared to have everything under control. Andrea observed with awe as Mo presided over the fast-paced preparations. She wondered how she would ever absorb the myriad of details involved in the business.

Lee, the nighttime hostess, stuck her head in the kitchen door. "Mo, can you come to the lobby for a second?"

Following her friend into the foyer, Andrea's mouth sagged open at the sight of the breathtaking exotic flowers almost obscuring the young woman delivering them.

"Holy guacamole! Who died?" Mo exclaimed.

"These are for Maureen Callaway," came a small voice from behind the massive arrangement. "Where do you want 'em?"

Mo pointed to the desk. The young woman set the vase down with a grateful sigh and extended a clipboard for her signature.

"Lee," she said, scribbling on the paper, "give this lady a nice tip. I'd say she earned at least five bucks for lugging this jungle in here."

Andrea sidled up beside Mo and gave her a nudge. "Well, well. I thought you said Christopher was the only man in your life these days."

"Shhhh," Mo hissed, smacking her away and ripping open the tiny white envelope. She pulled out the card and drew back, looking puzzled.

"What does it say?" Andrea asked.

Mo scratched her head. "It says, *That ornery twin brother of mine ought to be horsewhipped for treating you so badly this afternoon. I look forward to introducing you to the nicer side of the family.* It's signed, Madison McKee. Who the hell is Madison McKee?"

Andrea's stomach jumped. "Oh!" she gasped. "That's the guy from lunch. I think they're for me."

Mo shrieked with laughter and pounded her head with the heel of one hand. "You haven't been in town twelve hours, and already you've got some guy chasing after you. What in the world did you do to deserve it?"

"I meant to tell you, but I didn't get around to it."

Mo's eyes twinkled with mischief. "Let's get back to the kitchen and you can give me the whole scoop."

Andrea cast one last look at the magnificent bouquet and followed Mo, aware that her heart was beating rapidly.

* * *

Madison swiveled around in his chair and watched the evening sun transform the glass high-rises into mirrors of gold. He glanced at his watch. Stephanie's plane from Tucson should be landing just about now. Normally, he looked forward to the vivacious brunette's visit, but today, for some strange reason, he wished he could cancel their dinner date.

He'd been agitated all afternoon—ever since his father dropped the bombshell about Sundial House. He rose and stood at the window, absent-mindedly drumming the sill. He'd really done it this time, jumped into it with both feet. How the hell was he going to extricate himself from this predicament? The easiest way would be to tell his father he'd changed his mind and suggest one of the other partners handle Russell Stanton's case. But when had he ever taken the easy way out? No, he admitted with a sigh, he'd given his word.

Church bells from the street below signaled six o'clock. As if drawn by an invisible force, his attention turned to the stately Victorian house four blocks away. Except for a handful of unremarkable buildings in the area, it stood alone, its steep gabled roof thrusting proudly toward the sky. He could appreciate why Maureen Callaway was reluctant to part with it. His pulse rate picked up as he thought of her for the hundreth time that afternoon.

He moved to the desk and snapped his briefcase shut. If he hurried, he had time to stop by Sundial House. A smile twitched at the corners of his mouth. The flowers should have arrived by now, and hopefully the enclosed note achieved the desired effect.

In the underground garage, Madison climbed into his new hunter-green Range Rover and drove out. His palms grew damp as he neared the restaurant. Did he dare admit to himself that it wasn't the business aspect that had his nerves on edge?

He pulled up to the curb, but made no move to get out.

Perhaps coming here wasn't a good idea. Stephanie would be expecting him. But after another moment's hesitation, he shut the engine off. The insistent pull to see Maureen Callaway again was undeniable. His heart twisted as he remembered how his harsh words had brought a look of distress to her almond-shaped eyes, how her fingers had trembled.

This was absurd. He could't allow personal feelings to interfere with such a sensitive business matter. He thought he was a master at that. He gave an exasperated groan, but before he could change his mind again, he leaped out and strode inside. A petite, auburn-haired woman greeted him with a friendly smile.

He smiled back. "I'm Madison McKee. Is Ms. Callaway in? I don't have an appointment, but I wanted to make sure the flowers arrived," he said, eyeing the giant bouquet.

"I'll see if she's available," she said, tossing him a speculative glance over her shoulder as she rushed from the room.

Balancing a tray of empty stemware, Andrea jumped away with a gasp as the door suddenly swung open in her face.

"Guess what?" Lee announced in a conspiratorial tone. "The guy who sent the flowers is here!" She clapped her palms together beneath her chin, as Andrea and Maureen stared at each other. "Is he ever cute."

Andrea set the tray down, unable to trust the tremor in her hands.

"So, what do I tell him?" Lee prodded.

"Show him into the lounge," Mo instructed.

Andrea's feet felt glued to the floor. It was an effort to swallow. Did she or didn't she want to see him? Oh, my God, I'm a mess, she thought visualizing her drab appearance.

Head cocked to one side, Mo planted fists on her hips.

"What are you waiting for? Go out and thank the man for the flowers."

"Is my mascara smudged?"

Mo's eyes had a wicked gleam. "I thought you said you weren't interested? And no, your mascara isn't smudged. Quit fussing, and get out there."

Andrea caught the curious looks from the cook and his assistant. She smoothed back her hair and drew in a deep breath before walking out of the kitchen.

She paused in the doorway of the dimly-lit lounge, her eyes searching the room. When her gaze connected with Madison McKee's, her stomach went cold. Nervously, she jammed her hands into her jean pockets as he rose from his chair and approached her.

"Hi," he said softly.

The candlelight made his chestnut hair gleam with reddish overtones. With difficulty, she found her tongue. "Hello."

"Did the flowers meet with your approval?"

"They're beautiful. I enjoyed the note too." She surprised herself by adding, "Are you the good twin?"

His dimples deepened as his lips spread over even white teeth. "Sure am. The ornery one sends his heartfelt apology though."

Andrea laughed. "Apology accepted."

Madison felt a rush of comfort at her receptive manner and wished he didn't have to leave. Perhaps the negotiations wouldn't be so bad after all. Attempting a businesslike tone, he said, "I would like to schedule a meeting with you at my office, if that's convenient."

For a moment, Andrea was nonplussed, then she remembered the mix-up. "Mr. McKee, there's a little matter we need to clear up. I'm not Maureen Callaway. My name is Andrea Dusseaux." She extended her hand.

Madison took it. Her touch sent a strong vibration up his arm as he grappled with feelings of surprise and relief.

"Andrea Dusseaux," he repeated, allowing her name to linger on his lips. He felt as though he were drowning in the blue ocean of her eyes.

As his hand tightened around hers, Andrea felt a fire igniting her cheeks. Thank God he couldn't see her blushing in this low light. She heard Mo's voice behind her and quickly withdrew her hand and stepped aside to introduce them. *"This* is Maureen Callaway, my best friend."

Maureen hooked an arm through Andrea's. "I don't usually like lawyers, Mr. McKee," she said, addressing him with a teasing grin, "but because you have such good taste in flowers, I'd be willing to make an exception."

"Mr. McKee needs to talk with you about something," Andrea said.

The remark about lawyers was not lost on Madison. He realized he was treading on no less dangerous ground than before. All of a sudden he was glad he had the dinner date with Stephanie. He needed time to think.

"I have a small matter to discuss with you, Ms. Callaway. May I call you tomorrow?" He noted the thoughtful glint in her eyes and was careful to maintain a friendly smile.

"Sure."

"So nice to have met you both." He gave them a nod, then wheeled around and strode out the front door.

Andrea went hollow with confusion.

Mo mirrored her puzzled expression. "Was it something I said?"

In Mo's tiny bedroom, Andrea shifted her position on the rug and leaned against the side of the chenille-covered bed. She watched Mo cross-legged on the floor opposite her rummaging in the nearly empty potato chip bag and shook her head. "Look at us. Two sophisticated thirty-one year old women of the world, and here we are sitting on the floor with champagne and chips."

"Bite your tongue! You be thirty-one. I'm staying twenty-nine the rest of my life," Mo said with mock severity, draining her drink.

"Then so am I." Andrea raised her empty glass in salutation, then sighed and grew pensive.

"What's wrong?"

"Oh, nothing. I was just thinking that after you left college it was never the same. All the excitement vanished."

"Well, if you hadn't been in such a hurry to marry Dr. Wonderful . . ."

"I wish I could go back and start over."

Mo clambered unsteadily to her feet. "Hold that thought. I'm going to get some more snacks and another one of these," she said, waving the empty champagne bottle.

"I don't know if that's a good idea. Looks to me like you couldn't pass a sobriety test."

"Watch me touch my nose," she said, playfully poking her finger into her cheek. They giggled as Maureen padded from the room.

Andrea rose and moved to the open window framed by flowered cotton curtains. Bright moonlight glinted off the swing-set in the tree-draped back yard. She pressed her nose against the screen and the scent of jasmine from the vines nearby wafted toward her. She closed her eyes and deeply inhaled the sweet fragrance as her thoughts trailed back over her life. If she could go back, where would she start?

"Ta Dah! Second course" Mo stood in the doorway, champagne bottle in hand. She tossed a bag of Cheese Doodles to Andrea.

"This is the life!" she exclaimed with a laugh, catching the bag.

"Shhhhh. We'd better keep it down or we'll wake Christopher."

With pillows wedged firmly behind them, they settled

again on the floor between the two twin beds. Mo popped the champagne open and refilled the glasses. "Okay. On to serious stuff. I can guess what one of your biggest regrets is. Marrying ol' what's-his-face when you'd only known him for three weeks."

Andrea shrugged. "So, I wasn't thinking clearly."

"More like your brain took a hiatus."

"It's hard to explain how I was feeling."

A twinkle appeared in Mo's eyes. "Could it have been sheer unadulterated lust?"

"Hardly." Andrea averted her gaze and wondered how she could put into words the misery she'd suffered those eight years with Bernard.

"If it wasn't lust then it had to be the fact that he was a madly successful plastic surgeon who lived in a fabulous mansion in upstate New York and vacationed in Europe ten times a year."

Andrea stared blankly at Mo. "That wasn't it either."

"Then what was it? The man had a personality like a bowl of warm pudding."

"Dad had just died. I don't know, it felt right at the time."

"Freud would say it was a father replacement."

"Oh, stop. He was nothing of the sort."

"I'll tell you what he was. Weird, that's what! The man reinvented himself, changed his name, disowned his family and then ran out and got himself a beautiful wife half his age. Admit it, you were the ultimate possession, just like one of those expensive pieces of art he had decorating the place."

Mo had hit very close to home, Andrea thought ruefully. "He had some good points."

"I can't think of what they could be," she sniffed. "And God knows he was the vainest man I ever met. I wonder how much alteration he did on his own face!"

Andrea cringed inside. "Oh, come off it, Mo! When you

start exaggerating there's no stopping you." She took a sip of her drink, then absently traced the rim of the glass. "He wasn't always like that. He was kind and caring at the beginning and I really thought he loved me. He came along when I was at my lowest point, and maybe I mistook my feelings of gratitude for love."

"You know the thing that blew me away when I came to visit? That you two had separate bedrooms!"

"Bernard had insomnia and he didn't want to keep me awake at night," she countered defensively.

"Bull! Quit making excuses for him."

Andrea's stomach clenched as she realized that was exactly what she had done all those years—made excuses for him, while she'd come close to losing herself in the mannequin-like person she'd become. How could she tell Mo the intimate side of their life had been practically non-existent? It was too degrading to admit even to herself.

Bernard had also been adamant about not having children, in spite of her longing for them. Pregnancy would spoil her figure, make her unattractive, he'd explained. And children? They were messy little creatures, he'd said with disdain. All that would mar the picture-perfect image he wanted to portray to the rest of the world.

Mo cut in, as if she'd eerily zeroed in on her thoughts. "And to think he dropped you for that slut in his office he knocked up, and then had the gall to hold you to that stupid prenuptial agreement. I have to nominate him for creep of the century."

Andrea hastened to change the painful subject, allowing a valiant smile to crease her lips. "A picnic is supposed to be fun! Talking about Bernard is giving me indigestion. Of course, it could be the Cheese Doodles." She giggled and then raised her glass in a toast. "Here's looking forward to good things."

"Speaking of good things, that must be some wardrobe you got stuffed in those bags," Mo said, resting her elbow on one of the suitcases. "Why did you bring so much stuff for just three weeks?"

"The year's lease on the sublet was up, and my neighbor was willing to scatter my knickknacks and pictures around her studio apartment. But since her closet is about the size of a shoebox, the clothes had to make the trip with me."

"Where will you stay when you get back?"

"I'll cross that bridge when I get to it."

"That used to be my line . . . Ouch!" Mo cried, pressing her fingers into her temples.

"It's that headache again. Have you seen a doctor?"

"Yeah. He wants to give me a test, a brain scan or something, which brings me to another favor I have to ask you.

"Anything."

"The exam is scheduled for tomorrow at one. And when I checked the calendar earlier, I realized I'm supposed to attend a meeting at the City Planning Department at the same time. Do you think you could go in my place?"

"To which one? The test or the meeting?"

"Funny. Ha, ha."

"Okay, but that's the middle of the lunch hour. What about the restaurant?"

"Don't worry about that. Rose will be back tomorrow."

"At this meeting—do I take notes or something?"

"Yeah. I need to know what those weasels are up to."

Chapter Three

Madison impatiently shifted his weight on the metal chair and watched the slides flicking on and off the screen in the semi-darkness of the assembly room. After listening to the opposing views to Russell Stanton's project, he'd asked the committee to grant him an extension to study the case file before making his presentation.

Although he'd half expected Maureen Callaway to be there, he was relieved that she wasn't. Until this morning, he'd had no idea the meeting was scheduled. He'd hoped that they could get together privately before confronting each other in a public forum.

A sudden shaft of light from the hallway pierced the gloom as the door swung open revealing the outline of a woman. Damn. He'd spoken too soon. This was probably her now.

Andrea hesitated in the doorway of the darkened room. Hot and out of breath, she was annoyed with herself for arriving late. "Is this the Planning Department meeting?" she whispered to a man standing near the doorway.

"Yes." He pointed to the area beyond the silvery outline of a long table. "There are a couple of empty chairs over there. Watch out for the extension cords on the floor."

She thanked him as the door closed softly behind her, then stood still for a moment to allow her eyes to adjust to the darkness.

Guided by the intermittent light of the slide projector, she picked her way across the room where she spotted a vacant chair. Her heel snagged something. But before she could catch her balance, she felt herself falling as her purse hit the floor and the contents scattered.

She landed unceremoniously on her knees, her face wedged firmly between a man's muscular thighs. For a few seconds she knelt, disoriented, aware only of the scalding waves of embarrassment that washed over her.

"Are you all right?" asked a familiar voice.

Astonished, she drew her gaze upward. It couldn't be! "Oh my God!" she breathed. What was *he* doing here? Her eyes met the surprise in his.

Madison's cheek almost touched hers as he leaned close to whisper. "Hello again. I hate to spoil the moment, but you might find the chair a bit more comfortable."

Tongue-tied, Andrea struggled for composure and jumped as his hands encircled her waist. Gently, he guided her into the chair beside him.

"I'll help you find whatever you dropped when the lights go on," he murmured. His soft breath in her ear raised a host of goose bumps at the nape of her neck.

"Thank you."

Staring at the renderings on the screen, she was unable to make sense of anything. The stuffy room, combined with her embarrassment, made her feel as if her clothes were clinging to her like Saran Wrap.

She tried to concentrate on what was being said, but her mind insisted on replaying what she must have looked like tripping and diving forward into Madison McKee's lap. Of all places. An inopportune fit of giggles overtook her as she imagined every head in the room turn toward her. She bit the inside of her lip and pressed one fist to her mouth, in a vain attempt for control.

He leaned close. "A funeral."

"What?"

"Think of a funeral."

Although she appreciated his sense of humor, his remark did little to diminish the giddy feeling inside her. She was thankful she'd regained her composure by the time the slide show ended and the overhead lights flashed on. Everyone stood to leave.

"Here," said Madison, handing her some of the things that had fallen from her purse. "Did I find everything?"

"I think so." She met the glint of amusement in his eyes. "I'm surprised to see you here."

"No more than I'm surprised to see you."

"Maureen couldn't make it. Did I miss anything?"

He gave her a disarming smile. "Nothing that I can't fill you in on over dinner."

She paused. She'd only met this man yesterday. Was she ready for this? Part of her said no, but something made her want to recklessly say yes. She started to accept when a thin man with horn-rimmed glasses slapped him heartily on the shoulder.

"Hey, Madison! I didn't hear about you taking the case until this morning. Otherwise I would have sent the files to you sooner."

Andrea noticed Madison stiffen and a troubled look enter his eyes as he grabbed the man's arm and pulled him aside. "Listen, Scott, can I call you later?"

The man glanced over at her while raising an appreciative brow. "Oh! I got you," he said as if suddenly realizing he'd interrupted them. He pointed his forefinger like a pistol in Madison's direction as he backed toward the door. "Later, buddy. Hope you have better luck on this one than

I did. It's been a royal pain dealing with that witch at Sundial House!''

Andrea shot a glance at Madison and caught the stunned expression on his face. Suddenly, things were all too clear. The flowers. The invitation to dinner. She felt as if every drop of blood had drained from her head. She'd come very close to allowing herself to be manipulated again. Was this going to be a pattern in her life?

Mortified, Madison closed the distance between them. ''I'm sorry you had to hear that. I can explain.''

''Don't bother,'' she cut in icily. ''I think I understand all too well.'' She prayed he didn't notice the haze of tears in her eyes as she straightened her shoulders and marched from the room.

Shocked into uncommon silence, Madison wrestled with feelings of anger and regret. Why the hell did Scott have to make such a stupid remark? With a groan, he envisioned the impossible task ahead after Maureen learned of this. But more important, he needed to redeem himself with Andrea.

''Wait!'' he shouted, forcing his legs into action.

She didn't respond, only quickened her pace toward the elevator and smacked the down button.

He rushed to her side. ''Let me apologize for Scott's unprofessional remark,'' he said as the door slid open to reveal a packed elevator. She wedged herself in. Seeing it was unfeasible to squeeze in beside her, he held the door open. ''I'd appreciate your not mentioning this to Maureen just yet. And please, if you'll both join me for dinner, I can clarify everything.''

''I'll pass. Why don't you try asking her yourself?''

The door shut in his face.

Andrea was still inwardly fuming when she returned to Sundial House and stepped into the foyer where she was greeted by a rainbow of light streaming in from the stained glass windows.

"Maureen's on the phone," a waiter informed her, extending the receiver to her.

"Guess where I am?" Mo chirped on the line.

"Where?" she snapped. She wasn't in the mood for riddles.

"At the hospital, sitting on a cold chair with a draft blowing on my . . . *derrière.*"

Andrea felt a stab of guilt. In her anger, she'd forgotten all about Mo's visit to the doctor. "You didn't say anything about a hospital."

"Neither did my doctor. He wants to keep me overnight for more tests."

"What's going on?" she asked, alarmed.

"Don't worry, he says it's routine. Whoops! Someone's here to take me to X-ray. Listen, I need a couple of things."

Andrea grabbed a pencil from the reception desk and jotted down the items Mo requested. "I'll bring them right over."

"No, Manuel can do it. I'd rather you pick up Christopher from school." She gave Andrea the address. "Oh, and another thing. The babysitter has classes so would you mind filling in for her tonight?"

"Of course not! It will give me a chance to finally spend some time with him."

"By the way, how did the meeting go?"

Andrea suppressed the urge to blurt out the bizarre turn of events. "I only caught the tail end. Anyway, you've got to go. I'll tell you everything tomorrow."

Andrea's emotions were in turmoil as she cradled the phone. Was Mo worse than she let on? She tightened her jaw as Madison's face crept into her thoughts. How could he have been so blatantly deceitful, pretending to be interested in her when his real intentions were to further his own agenda? The worst part of it was that she had believed him. Her hand curled around the reservation book, and she had to stop herself from hurling it across the foyer.

She grabbed the list Mo had given her and went to the back to find Manuel, almost welcoming the distraction that would keep her from thinking of that self-serving cad.

Madison reached for the phone and pushed the numbers for Sundial House. "Andrea Dusseaux, please."

"She's not here right now. This is Rose. May I help you?"

"It's personal. When do you expect her back?"

"Are you calling from New York?"

He hesitated. He hated to lie, but he doubted she'd be forthcoming with any information if he didn't.

"Yes, I'm a friend."

"She won't be back this evening. She has to stay home and take care of Christopher."

"Christopher?" Somehow he hadn't pictured her with a son. He realized that other than her name, he knew nothing about the woman who had captured his imagination.

"Maureen's son. She's at the hospital."

"Nothing serious, I hope."

"No, just in for tests overnight. Do you need the home number?"

"I think I have it right here," he said, reaching for the Sundial House file on his desk.

He hung up, located Maureen's personal information and was about to dial when all of a sudden he changed his mind. He had a better idea.

"Do you want me to show you how to play checkers now, Andie?" Christopher asked expectantly, setting the pieces on the board while sitting cross-legged on the green and orange braided rug that covered the hardwood floor in the living room.

"Yes, I'd like to, but how about some dinner first?"

"Kool-aid and potato chips."

She smiled to herself and thought, he's a junk food junkie just like his mother. "Tell you what. I make a great grilled cheese. Will you have one with me?"

He looked mildly disappointed. "Okay. But, can we play right after?"

"Scouts' honor." She studied his serious little face and his long-lashed blue eyes, greatly magnified by thick steel-rimmed glasses. He'd been concerned about his mother until Mo called and convinced him that it was nothing serious. Andrea fervently hoped that was true. The doorbell chimed as she started for the kitchen.

"I'll get it," Christopher shouted.

"No, you go wash those grubby hands before we eat."

She sent him off with a gentle pat to his behind and moved to the front door, slipping the chain lock on before pulling it open. She froze in surprise.

Madison McKee stood on the porch in the fading light of the setting sun, a solicitous smile on his face. Her first reaction was to slam the door shut.

She tried to convince herself that she wasn't glad to see him, but her racing pulse belied that. "What are you doing here?"

He held out a bottle of wine in one hand and a large paper bag in the other. "Paté or pizza?"

Chapter Four

"Yeah! Pizza!"

Andrea jumped, unaware that Christopher had come up behind her and wedged his face into the narrow opening.

"Hi, Christopher. My name is Madison McKee." He gave him a broad smile.

"Are you Andie's friend?"

Madison gave her a provocative stare. "Andie may not think so, but I could be."

She couldn't decide whether she was irritated that he'd taken the liberty of using her nickname, or was amused by his obvious ploy to charm her through the boy.

"How did you know Christopher's name?"

"Nothing is impossible if you're interested enough to find out."

"Maureen isn't here," she said, keeping her voice steady.

"I know."

"Of course. You seem to know everything."

He gave her a sly grin. "Actually, I called Sundial House

and Rose was kind enough to fill in some of the blanks."
He glanced at the paper bag. "So. Do we get to eat inside,
or do we picnic on the porch?"

"What kind of pizza are we eating?" Christopher asked
with interest.

"Pepperoni."

"My favorite!" He jumped up and down, clapping his
hands.

Andrea realized she'd lost control of the situation. The
pizza was now a firm bond between the two. She gave
Madison a reproachful look and, with a sigh, unchained
the door.

Christopher happily zigzaged around the mis-matched
living room furniture and pranced through the arched
doorway to the small dining alcove, gesturing for Madison
to follow him. "Here," he said, jumping onto a chair and
smacking the tabletop. "We always eat here when we have
company."

Andrea noticed the smug look on Madison's face.
"Chalk one up to the bad guys," she said just loud enough
for him to hear.

He thought of a clever comeback, but decided against
it. He set the wine on the antique pine table and opened
the pizza box.

Christopher started to grab a piece. "Ooh, it's hot!" he
said, flapping his fingers.

"Wait, honey, I'll get you a plate," she said.

Madison swiftly pulled paper plates, napkins and forks
from the bag. "If you'll get the glasses and something to
open the wine, I have everything else."

She rested her hands on her hips. "You must do this a
lot."

"Not since my college days."

"Oh? And where was that?" she asked offhandedly.

"Harvard."

"My old neighborhood."

"One more thing to bring us even closer." He gave her a knowing glance.

She headed for the refuge of the kitchen, hoping he hadn't noticed the flush that heated her face. She knew he was alluding to the fall that had landed her head first in his lap. Visualizing the moment made her giggle as she threw open several cupboards to search for wine glasses. She found two and then paused. Oh, God! What would Mo think if she knew her adversary was under her own roof?

Returning to the dining room with the glasses and a cold can of soda for Christopher, she stopped abruptly in the doorway. And what would Mo think of him casually sharing a pizza with her son? The sight of the boy's animated face and the sound of their laughter dispelled any notion she may have entertained to cut the visit short. Madison had her backed into a corner. She composed her features as she approached.

"Allow me." He jumped up to pull out her chair. Undetected, he cast an appreciative glance at her as she sat. He liked the way the denim shorts hugged her shapely thighs.

The man was using his charm for all it was worth, she thought, suppressing a smile as he picked up the wine bottle, extracted the cork and poured.

He moved to sit opposite her and immediately served a slice of pizza to Christopher who eyed it expectantly. "I hope you like pepperoni too," he said, carefully sliding a piece onto Andrea's plate.

"I do, but don't think that this battle can be won with a pizza."

"Of course not. That's why I sprang for the paté," he said, pointing to the unopened container.

Andrea laughed.

Encouraged, he raised his glass to her. "Truce?"

"For the time being." She took a sip, savoring the full-bodied Beaujolais.

"So, how are things in the Big Apple these days?" he asked.

She arched a brow in surprise. "What else do you know about me?"

"Not nearly enough."

To mask her embarrassment, Andrea slid another slice of pizza onto Christopher's plate, although he'd barely finished the first one.

"Are you relocating to Phoenix?" Madison inquired.

She tossed her head back. "No. Just visiting for three weeks."

"I thought you were working with Mommy," Christopher said, pulling a string of cheese into the air.

"Your Mommy's teaching me."

Madison picked up the cue. "Are you opening a restaurant in New York?"

"That might be in the distant future."

"I suppose you have someone there to help you?"

"Is this fishing expedition going anywhere?" she asked in mock confrontation.

"Yes. Are you married?"

"Not anymore. You?"

He looked guarded as if surprised that she'd turned the tables on him. "Engaged once."

Before Andrea could dwell on his answer, Christopher piped up. "Can I have another piece?"

"What's all this?" she asked, pointing to the mound of crusts on his plate.

Christopher looked petulant. "I don't like the crust."

Madison leaned over toward the boy. "Want to know a secret? I don't either," he whispered in a conspiratorial tone, serving him another slice.

"I don't see you leaving any on your plate," she teased.

He gave her a defiant look. "I'm on my best behavior tonight."

Andrea smiled, reluctant to admit to herself that she found him utterly charming.

"Andie, are you going to take me to my Little League game tomorrow?"

"No. Your mommy will be back by then."

"If her head isn't hurting again," he mumbled, looking dejected.

She reached out and smoothed a strand of hair from his forehead. "I'm sure the doctors are finding out what's wrong at the hospital right now and they'll make her better."

Madison leaned the chair back on two legs. "So, Christopher, where do you play ball?"

"Encanto Park."

Andrea munched on paté and crackers as the two bantered back and forth about baseball. Christopher seemed to be enjoying the unexpected company. She wondered if he missed not having a father and felt a twinge of jealousy when he asked Madison to play checkers instead of her.

When all the pizza had been devoured, as well as half the paté and crackers, Christopher excitedly pulled Madison into the living room.

Andrea watched them with interest while she cleared the table. Madison's gentle patience with the boy almost made her forget that he was a devious and calculating attorney. He looked perfectly comfortable sitting on the floor in his blue jeans and open-collared shirt. Behind them on the end table the enormous vase of flowers he'd sent her made a colorful backdrop.

She chose a chair nearby and leafed through a magazine while observing him over the top of the page. He seemed to have a gift for getting down to a child's level, judging by the rapturous expression on Christopher's face.

As if he knew she was evaluating him, he looked up and gave her an intimate smile that made her pulse throb in her temples. She averted her eyes. She could not permit

herself to be attracted to this man. Due to the awkward
circumstances, there was little chance of anything developing between them.

In an attempt to assert herself, she set the magazine
aside. "Christopher, it's time for bed. We've kept Mr.
McKee long enough."

"Please. Madison's fine by me."

Christopher looked crushed. "Just one more game.
Please, Andie. Please?"

"You promised your mother on the phone you'd go to
bed at eight and it's already twenty after. Come on."

He threw Madison a pleading look, obviously hoping to
enlist his support.

"Young man, a promise is a promise." Madison gathered
the checkers into the box. "But I'd like a rematch. You
beat me so many games tonight."

Christopher giggled and playfully punched Madison's
arm. "I bet I can beat you again."

"We'll see."

"Okay!" The look of sheer delight on the boy's face
made Andrea's heart turn over. He was adorable. As she
watched him leave the room, she felt a renewed longing
for a child of her own.

Madison rose and moved to her side. "I need to understand a few things about Maureen. May I stay awhile and
talk?"

The thought of being alone in the room without Christopher as a buffer sent a thrill of uncertainty through her.
At the same time, she was reluctant to discuss Mo with
him. "Well . . . it is late and I . . ."

"Fifteen minutes?"

"I have to put Christopher to bed."

"Take your time." He eased into a chair and pulled a
magazine from the coffee table.

Christopher appeared in the doorway in his pajama bot-
toms. "Andie, are you going to tuck me in?"

"Of course. Tell Mr . . . um . . . Madison thank you for the pizza."

"Thanks," he said, padding over to Madison. "You won't forget about the checkers?"

"Not on your life." He ruffled the boy's hair. "Goodnight." He watched them leave hand in hand, then laid the magazine down and took a good look around.

The room, with its uneven plaster walls and paint peeling from the high ceiling, was no improvement from the crumbling walkway and cracked shingles outside. Maureen Callaway was obviously short on cash. So why the devil was she rejecting the lucrative offers for her property?

When Andrea returned and joined him on the couch, he noted her fidgeting nervously.

"What do you want to know about Maureen?" she asked stiffly.

"I'd like to understand what I'm dealing with here. Why is she turning down the offer? For that amount she could afford to relocate her business in a better section of town and live in a much nicer house."

"To you things are all numbers on a page. It's not always about dollars, you know."

"What is it then? Is there a buried treasure on the property? More than double your original investment in five years is not a bad deal."

"It would take more than fifteen minutes to try and make you understand."

He spread his arms across the back of the couch. "You have my attention for as long as it takes."

Andrea felt annoyed, realizing that she'd now entrapped herself. She questioned the wisdom of interfering in Mo's private business. "I still think Maureen is the one you should be talking to."

"You're her friend. If I had a better idea where she's coming from, maybe I could find a solution that would help her."

"And, of course, helping her is your *only* motive," she said sarcastically.

He studied her in silence. She had that same look of hostility as in their first encounter. "You're treating me as if I'm the enemy. I'm not. I'd like to negotiate this situation to the satisfaction of both parties. I wish you could trust me on that."

"Trust you? Funny request from someone who tried to hide the fact that he was buttering me up to get to Mo."

His jaw tightened. "You'll find this hard to believe, but when we met I had no idea that this case was going to fall in my lap. I didn't relish taking it on. I was pressured."

"And, of course, the lucrative fee involved didn't enter your mind."

He gave her a level look. "It's not always about dollars, as you already pointed out. My involvement with this case is probably as personal as yours with Maureen."

Andrea read the sincerity in his eyes. "Then you can understand that it's not easy to pull up roots when you'd never had them before."

"You realize that if she doesn't sell, if this deal falls through and they decide to move this project elsewhere, it will be a damaging blow to property in this area. With all due respect to the good business she has going, the neighboring houses are more or less in the shape this place is in. And as the area declines, so will the business."

Andrea knew he made sense. "What do you expect from me?"

"I need to convince her that this deal would be beneficial for both her and Christopher. And now that she's undoubtedly angry with me about Scott's remark, I need your help."

"I haven't told her yet."

His look of surprise quickly changed into a smile. "I hope you'll put in a good word for me when you do. And now, let's set business aside." He folded his arms. "I think you owe me an apology."

"Why is that?"

"For assuming my interest in you is only to sway the outcome of this case."

"I'd take that as a compliment, but you don't know anything about me."

"I'd like to rectify that."

Andrea avoided his gaze and rose from the couch, feeling uncomfortable and confused. Why was she fighting her obvious attraction to this man?

"Maureen will be home tomorrow," she said, moving toward the door. "I'll see what I can do."

Realizing he was being dismissed, Madison rose to join her at the open door. He walked outside, then turned back to her. "Have you ever stepped into a postcard?"

"What?"

"Take a look," he said, gesturing behind him.

Andrea followed him onto the porch and stared at the giant yellow moon suspended over the rooftops across the street. There were no words to describe it.

He watched her expression of awe. The bright moonlight illuminated her hair which framed her face like a silver halo. She looked like an angel.

He noted her arms folded tightly in front of her as though she were creating an impermeable barrier. Overwhelmed by the desire to touch her, he reached out and smoothed a strand of hair away from her face.

Andrea flinched and moved to the porch railing. Why had she overreacted to such a casual gesture? If it had been anybody else, she wouldn't have given it a second thought. But her stong feelings for him warned her to be careful. She wasn't ready for a situation she might not be able to handle.

He moved to stand beside her, looking puzzled. "I get the feeling that I frighten you."

She quickly assumed the placid demeanor, the one that

she'd hidden behind for so many years. "Do I have any reason to be?"

He grinned. "No. I'm just a simple cowboy at heart."

"I would never have pegged you for that." Even as she said it, she realized it wasn't so hard to imagine. Discreetly, she admired his unpretentious attire and once again pictured him sprawled on the floor with Christopher.

"When I was growing up, all this didn't exist," he said gesturing toward the canyon of high-rises only a few blocks away. "We had a ranch in west Phoenix just ten miles from here. Back then, I could rope a steer with the best of them." He slouched against the corner post. "If you're free tomorrow evening we could take a drive. I'd very much like to show you the town, and to be honest, I'd love to see you again."

She turned to face him squarely, her heart beating hard, and was startled by the look of tenderness on his face. Involuntarily, her gaze trailed to his lips, almost willing them to come closer.

Drawn by the invitation in her eyes, he bent his head, tentatively touching his lips to the side of her mouth, aware of his own pounding heart.

She held her breath, surprised by the desire he ignited in her. As if it were the most natural thing in the world, she turned her face to receive his kiss, soft, gently exploring. Suddenly, all she was aware of was the moonlight, the heady scent of jasmine and the sensation that her knees were threatening to fold.

When she felt his arms encircle her waist, she drew away, feeling flustered. "I have to go in now."

Madison was slightly baffled by her sudden withdrawal, but hid his concern. "How about that drive tomorrow?"

"I don't know."

"Will you sleep on it?"

"Okay."

He squeezed her hand, then turned and walked to his car.

After that kiss, Andrea thought, she'd be lucky if she slept at all.

Was it the remnants of jet lag, or the restless night that got her out of bed at the crack of dawn? Andrea wondered as she took her second cup of coffee onto the creaky porch. She sat down carefully in one of the splintery wooden chairs, leaned her head back and breathed in the cool air. She watched the progress of an industrious bumble bee among the tall irises poking their purple heads under the porch railings.

As hard as she tried, she couldn't get Madison's kiss out of her mind. What had possessed her to allow it to happen, to want it to happen? Under different circumstances, or at least if she were back home in New York, she could entertain the possibility of something more developing between them.

But why was she making such a big fuss over a kiss? Was it deeper than the simple surface explanation she was giving herself? The truth was that she was afraid to let her guard down, afraid to allow her heart to be trampled on again. For the past year she'd kept any possible suitors at arm's length, and yet, the mere recollection of Madison's face pulverized her apprehension. Oh Andie, you can't let this happen, she admonished herself. You're not a teen-ager looking for a holiday romance. Besides, what about Mo?

She set her empty cup at her feet and rose to stretch her legs, moving toward the porch railing, each step producing a groan from the aged timber. She looked out over the city.

Shafts of golden sunlight filtered through the palm trees which stretched against the bright sapphire sky, their lacy fronds swaying in the gentle breeze like giant dustmops, accentuating what must have once been a majestic neighborhood, now reduced to a shadow of itself. Madison was right. What would happen if the development moved elsewhere?

She had to persuade Mo to set aside her emotions and look at the situation objectively. She knew Mo's motivation stemmed from her unsettled childhood as the only daughter of a globe-trotting ambassador. It explained her fierce sense of possessiveness and pride about Sundial House. It was as though she were trying to prove to her dead father she could achieve the stability that he never expected from the daughter who was the mirror of himself. Ironically, Mo used the inheritance he'd left her to lay down the roots he could never give her.

A glance at her watch reminded Andrea that it was time to wake Christopher for school. She stepped inside, surprised at the eagerness she felt at the prospect of seeing the boy's impish face. She had to admit that with all the challenges that confronted Mo, her friend was lucky to have what she herself had been denied in her marriage to Bernard—a child.

Chapter Five

Andrea finished setting out the flatware in the main dining room as Rose had instructed her and was absorbed in arranging the napkins in a fluted pattern, when Mo's voice from the doorway made her jump. She swung around. "What are you doing here! I didn't expect you until after lunch." She curbed the desire to suggest she shouldn't have come in at all. Mo didn't look her usual rosy self.

"I escaped when no one was looking," she quipped, striding into the room, her ankle-length flowered dress flowing behind her. "Any major catastrophes waiting for me?"

Andrea's first thought was how she should break the news about Madison. "Rose tells me everything is under control here. But, what about you? What were the test results?"

Mo shrugged. "Won't know till this afternoon." She motioned for Andrea to follow her to the office, closed the door behind them and moved to the desk, where she stood leafing through a mound of papers. She turned and flashed a playful smile. "So what's up, kiddo? Did we get another visit from Madison?"

Andrea caught the teasing note. "As a matter of fact . . . we did," she began gingerly.

"Then how come you look so glum? We're talking about the best looking guy who's come down the pike in I don't know when. He's charming, sends flowers and he's probably filthy rich. What more can you ask for?"

"I'm quite aware of his attributes," she said, sitting on the couch and nervously smoothing the material of her beige slacks, wondering where to start.

"Hey. If you're waiting for my permission, you've got it. I don't expect you to spend every night you're here with me and Christopher." She turned her attention back to the blizzard of papers on her desk. "You know, you'd make a great looking couple. Kind of like Ken and Barbie," she said with a giggle.

Each word of praise compounded Andrea's feelings of guilt. How was she going to tell her? She shifted uncomfortably in her seat.

"Oh, by the way," Mo said, looking relieved as she extracted a folder from the bottom of the pile, "you were going to tell me about the meeting yesterday."

Andrea chewed the inside of her lip. "I found out there's a new attorney representing the Stanton project."

"Oh, God!" Mo cried, slapping the folder down. "Now I'll have to deal with one more idiot."

"Not necessarily," Andrea said uneasily. "You tell me to have an open mind. Why don't you take your own advice for a change?"

"Did you meet him?"

"Yes."

"And . . . ?"

Andrea gave a big sigh. "It's Madison Mckee."

Mo's face blanched. She plopped into her chair, pressed

two fingers to her temple and closed her eyes. "I should have known he was too good to be true."

"Come on. You can at least talk to him. Maybe you're overlooking a few important factors."

Mo's eyes popped open. "I take it the two of you have been discussing the ins and outs of my business."

Andrea threw her a severe look. "You know me better than that. But, what's the harm of listening to him? A minute ago he was God's gift to the world."

"You, more than anyone, should know how much this place means to me."

"I do, but . . ." A loud knock on the door interrupted her.

Benny, the cook, stuck his head in. "Excuse me, didn't you order salmon steaks for tonight's rehearsal dinner?"

"Of course I did," Mo snapped. "Didn't the Clover guy show up with the delivery?"

"He's here right now. He's brought chicken for a hundred people, not salmon."

Rose came up behind Benny. "A Mr. Wilson says he has an eleven o'clock appointment with you, Mo."

"Oh, my God! Cut me some slack, would you, people? I can only handle one disaster at a time. Jesus, my head is killing me!"

Rose and Benny exchanged a knowing look and withdrew wordlessly.

Andrea waited until Mo had calmed down. "I won't talk to Madison again if it's going to bother you this much."

"Don't be silly. Of course you can talk to him. Just don't talk about me." She paused, looking uncertain. "I'm sorry, Andie, I'm not trying to be difficult. Look, can we discuss this later? Somehow I've got to get hold of a hundred salmon steaks by six o'clock."

Andrea rose and draped an arm around Mo's shoulder. "Is there anything I can do to help?"

Mo pulled away with a sigh and began fanning through

the Rolodex. "I don't know." Her shoulders slumped as she glanced back at Andrea. "There is something. Seems like all I've done is impose on you, but could you take Christopher to his Little League game for me this afternoon?"

She smiled. "It's not an imposition. I'd love to."

Andrea left the office, realizing there was no easy way out of her predicament. Her heart twisted uncomfortably at the thought of not seeing Madison again, but she couldn't allow her feelings for him to come between her and Mo. All the better, she told herself, once again resurrecting the barrier that Madison's kiss had threatened to tear down.

From her perch on the fourth row of the bleachers, Andrea shaded her eyes against the sun and watched Christopher round third base and slide into home plate in a cloud of yellow dust. She jumped to her feet along with the other people in the stands and clapped her hands, yelling and screaming to the second runner following close on his heels. The burst of maternal pride that swept over her made her giddy. It was a good feeling pretending this little boy was hers, a feeling marred only by her decision not to see Madison again. Perhaps he'd had second thoughts too. Last night he seemed eager, but today, he had not called by the time she'd left Mo's house for Christopher's school.

Amid the enthusiastic congratulations of his teammates, Christopher cast a look of unabashed pride in her direction, which once again lifted her spirits. She gave him a wide smile and signaled a thumbs up.

The next batter struck out and the opposing team took the field. Andrea sat and fished in her purse for a pack of Lifesavers. She looked up as someone settled beside her and stifled the gasp of surprise as she stared straight into

Madison Mckee's warm brown eyes. A shiver of unexpected delight shot through her.

"Hi." His tone was intimate.

"Hi," she answered, responding automatically to his engaging smile, but quickly looked away as thoughts of Mo intruded. Acutely aware of his nearness, she struggled to find the right words to verbalize her decision regarding their impossible situation.

He leaned back and loosened his tie. "I tried calling the restaurant several times."

"You couldn't have tried too hard because I was there until three o'clock." She chided herself immediately. On the one hand, she was convinced she wanted nothing more to do with him, yet on the other, she was irritated that he hadn't called.

"I apologize. I was tied up in court all day and everytime I got a second to call, the line was busy."

"How did you know I was here?"

"When I finally got through, Rose told me you were taking care of Christopher again because Mo had some sort of emergency at the restaurant, and since last night Christopher mentioned where he'd be . . ."

"And what was your point in coming here?"

"We discussed going for a ride this evening, remember?"

"I didn't say I would."

"You also didn't say you wouldn't." He watched her fold her arms and turn away. Was he being too persistent? Had he perhaps moved too fast last night when he kissed her? But he wouldn't have, had he not sensed she wanted him to. "I get the feeling you're not too happy to see me."

Andrea turned to face him. "It's not you," she said with a sigh.

Then it dawned on him. "You talked with Maureen."

She gave a solemn nod. "She was less than thrilled to hear that we were discussing her behind her back."

"I'm sorry. It looks as though I have you caught in the crossfire."

"She's got a lot on her mind right now, but I'm pretty sure she'll agree to listen to what you have to say before rejecting it."

"I can hardly wait for the privilege," he said ruefully. He rested his elbows on his knees and laced his fingers together.

Andrea drew back and studied his chiseled profile. "By the way, last night you said this case affected you personally. What did you mean?"

He dipped his head, then looked up again, staring straight ahead as though focusing on some distant object far beyond the boundaries of the tree-filled park. "How's this for starters? The Stantons and McKees are fast friends until Yours Truly breaks his engagement to Russell's daughter, Victoria, after the wedding invitations are in the mail. The ensuing fallout consists of Victoria's mother having a nervous breakdown in addition to the permanent rift that was forged between the two families." He turned to meet her gaze. "My father approached me two days ago. If I can persuade your friend to stop blocking Russell's project, I get to be a hero."

Andrea nodded slowly. "And heal the rift, and set everything right again." Would that include resuming the relationship with Stanton's daughter? she wondered, feeling an inexplicable flash of jealousy.

Excitement erupted in the bleachers, tearing her from her thoughts. She rose to her feet in time to see Christopher catch the fly ball for the last out of the game. Surrounded by his exuberant teammates, he raised the ball for Andrea to see. She clambered down and rushed onto the field with all the parents.

Christopher's face lit up when he saw Madison behind her. "Hey, Madison, did you see me catch that ball?" he shrieked with excitement.

"I sure did." He ruffled the boy's matted blonde hair so hard, Christopher's glasses slid down to the end of his nose.

Andrea swooped the child up and twirled him around, pressing his flushed face to hers. She felt him stiffen. Realizing her action had probably embarrassed him in front of his friends, she quickly put him down.

"Get your things, Honey, it's time to go."

"But Mommy always lets me ride on the Merry-go-round before we go home."

It would have been easier to part with Madison now, but the pleading look on Christopher's dirt-smudged face made her give in. "All right, but we can't stay long."

"Whoopee!" Christopher shouted, waving his cap above his head. "Will you come watch me too, Madison?"

Madison shot a quick glance at Andrea to gauge her reaction, but her impassive expression gave him no clue. "Sure, apparently I don't have other plans for the evening." He noticed her flinch at his remark, then she took Christopher's hand and walked briskly ahead.

He followed them, feeling slightly disconcerted that his attempt to lighten the mood seemed to fall flat. She looked great in the pink blouse tucked neatly into snug blue jeans, he thought, watching the gentle sway of her hips. His heartbeat quickened at the memory of last night. She had returned his kiss with as much passion as he'd felt. About that, he had no doubt. Somehow he had to overcome the chasm that his forced association with Maureen Callaway had created. He felt an urgent need to be in Andrea's good graces again. He hurried to catch up with them as they entered the gate to the carnival where dozens of children had lined up for rides.

As Christopher whirled happily on the Merry-go-round to the tune of *The Yellow Rose of Texas,* Madison noticed Andrea turn sharply and focus her attention on the nearby tennis court where a lively doubles match was in progress.

He didn't miss the spark of interest that lit her wide blue eyes. "Do you play tennis?"

That brought a rueful grin to her face. "That's about all I did for eight years."

He folded his arms. "Fascinating."

She gave him a direct look. "That's not exactly what I would have called it."

What an odd thing to say, he thought. He wanted to know more, but decided this wasn't the time. "Listen. If you're interested, I can arrange a game of doubles at my club."

She gave him a sideways glance as if to say, 'you must be out of your mind.'

"I take it that's a no," he mumbled almost to himself as she returned her attention to Christopher.

A game of tennis would be heaven, Andrea thought. In addition to her love for the sport, it had always helped release her tension. Obviously, taking Madison up on his offer was out of the question under the circumstances. But she had to admire his nerve. She moved through the gate as the Merry-go-round came to a stop and lifted Christopher off his speckled pony. "I think you've had enough now. Give that poor horse a rest."

Christopher looked wistful. "I wish it *was* a real horse."

"I used to ride one when I was your age," Madison said joining in.

Christopher's eyes opened wide. "For real? Do you have a horse now?"

Madison bent down to face him. "Yes. I keep him at my sister's ranch in Sedona."

"Is that far?"

He shrugged. "Not very. I'm driving up this Sunday. She's got a lot more horses there."

"Wow! You think she'd let me come and ride one?"

The look of excited anticipation on the boy's face made Madison instantly regret his words. What was he thinking?

He cast a quick glance at Andrea and, sure enough, saw the irritation reflected in her eyes.

"Christopher," she said sharply. "Here, have one more ride." She pressed coins into the boy's eager hands and sent him off, then spun around to face Madison. "You know that's out of the question," she snapped, feeling anger heat her face. "What do you think you're doing, raising the boy's hopes like that?"

"Why should it be out of the question? I'd be delighted to have the three of you as my guests."

Andrea felt like screaming at the top of her lungs. "Were you born this way, or are you this pushy because you're a lawyer?"

Madison masked his annoyance. "Well, let me ask *you* something. Were you born this angry, or is this just for my benefit? I sensed your hostility when I first met you. Would you mind telling me what I've done to deserve such wrath?"

The fiery indignation in his eyes startled her. Deep down she knew he was right. "I'm sorry. Maybe I'm overreacting. But you must realize that this situation between you and Maureen has put me in an impossible spot."

"I apologize. I shouldn't have mentioned the horse."

"Let's hope Christopher can forget about it," she chided him gently.

"I guess after all this I don't dare ask you again about tonight."

"Definitely not tonight." She knew she should have said 'not tonight, or any other night.' Was she having second thoughts about not wanting to see him? It had seemed easy earlier, but now, standing beside him, unable to deny how attracted she was to him, she felt her resolve wavering. Her ambivalence disturbed her. How could she call him pushy when she was sending him mixed signals?

He felt encouraged. She'd said no, but somehow she'd left the door open. Cool it, Madison, he warned himself, don't press your luck.

"Well, I guess this is my cue to leave," he said politely. "I'll see you around, I hope." He waved to Christopher, then turned and walked away.

Andrea quelled her regret as she watched him leave, then moved to get Christopher.

"Where is Madison going?" he asked, jumping off the horse and craning his neck at the retreating figure.

"He remembered he had something important to do."

His face gathered in obvious disappointment. "What about riding the horse?"

"I'm sure your mother wouldn't approve. Maybe we'll find something else neat to do like the zoo or something," she said in a reassuring tone.

Her suggestion didn't erase the crestfallen look on his face. He shuffled his feet all the way to the car and said nothing on the short drive back to the house.

Maureen greeted them at the door. "Hi, guys. Who won the game?"

"Christopher drove in the winning run," Andrea announced proudly.

Mo knelt down and drew him into her arms. "That's my boy!"

Andrea's hopes that Christopher would forget Madison's invitation died when he ignored his mother's praise and said, "Guess what? Madison came to watch me play. And guess what? He says I can go horseriding with him on Sunday if you'll let me. Can I? Can I please?"

Mo shot Andrea a sharp look. "What's this all about?"

"I already told him it wasn't possible," she answered defensively.

"But, why can't I go, Mommy?" he whined.

Mo rose to her feet. "Because," she said sternly. "Go wash up for dinner. Now." Andrea was surprised at the harsh note in Mo's voice.

Christopher started to protest and then caught the look

of warning in his mother's eyes. Head bowed, he ambled down the hall to his room.

Mo turned to Andrea and spread her palms out. "I don't even want to know why Madison was there. I've got bigger problems to deal with."

Andrea's hand flew to her mouth. "Oh! The rehearsal dinner."

"Everything's under control there," she said with a dismissive wave, as she walked into the living room.

"Then what is it?" Andrea asked, setting her purse on the coffee table.

For a moment Mo said nothing, just stood staring out the wide picture window, her arms clasped tightly across her chest. "I got the test results from my doctor."

Her grave expression sent a shudder of apprehension through Andrea. She clutched her stomach which suddenly felt as if it was filled with ice. "What did he say?"

Her voice was flat. "I have a brain tumor."

Andrea moved to her side as if in a trance. "Are they sure?"

Mo gave her a tight-lipped nod.

"Oh, my God!"

Mo quickly pressed a finger to her lips. "Shhhh. I don't want Christopher to hear."

"I'm sorry." Confusion and fear gripped Andrea as she slid a limp arm around her friend's shoulder.

She let out a sigh. "The good news is there's a 50/50 chance that it's benign, but either way, it's gotta go. Now here's the problem. My doctor wants me to have laser surgery as soon as possible, and the three top specialists are in LA, Houston and New York."

"So what's the problem? Decide on one, and we'll go."

"Wait a minute." Mo drew back. "You can't go with me."

"Why not? You're the closest person I've got in the whole world. Like it or not, I'm going to stick to you like Velcro."

The flash of appreciation in Mo's eyes quickly dissolved into a sheen of tears. She turned her head away and pulled a tissue from her pocket. Andrea said nothing, sensing that she was fighting for control.

"What about Christopher?" Mo said in a choked voice. "Yesterday was the first night I've been away from him. Ever." She let that hang in the air for a moment. "I'd feel a whole lot better about going if I knew you were here with him."

"Why can't we both come?

"And have him hang around a hospital? He'd be scared out of his wits."

Andrea twirled the pearl ring her mother had given her around on her finger. "But I can't bear the thought of you going through surgery alone."

"I won't be alone. Listen, I've made five thousand calls in the last couple of hours and I've decided Houston would be best, mainly because Aunt Ethel is there."

"Didn't she go to London to get married?"

"She moved back to Houston last year with her husband. She's offered to stay with me in the hospital."

Andrea gave a resigned shrug. "When are you leaving?"

"This weekend. The specialist will want to run some more tests on Saturday, and if it's a go, he'll do the surgery first thing on Monday. I'll have Aunt Ethel call you the minute it's over."

Still plagued with doubt, Andrea let out a weary sigh. "You're your usual stubborn self," she said with mock severity. "Couldn't Rose stay with Christopher? I'd still feel better if I went along."

Mo's face softened. She wrapped Andrea in a tight embrace. "I know. And it means more to me than you could ever imagine." She pulled back and looked deep into Andrea's eyes. "The one thing that will give me peace of mind is knowing you'll be here."

Andrea nodded in acquiescence.

A wan smile creased Mo's face. "There's something else. If anything should happen to me . . ."

"Mo, stop it! You're being morbid. I spent hours at dinner parties talking to Bernard's cronies—top specialists most of them—and, from what I understand, laser surgery is much safer than the old way when they had to cut . . ." She quickly switched gears. "I'm going to think optimistically about this. You're going to be fine." She didn't miss the apprehension in Mo's tear-reddened eyes.

"What if it's not benign?"

The thought sent a searing pain through Andrea's heart and reminded her of the desolation she'd felt as a child when her mother died and then her father . . . To her Mo was the only semblance of family. "Don't."

"I have to be realistic, kiddo. Just in case things don't go right . . ." Her voice broke as the words tumbled out. "Promise me, you'll take care of Christopher."

Until that moment Andrea had deliberately sidestepped the possibility that the tumor could be malignant. She tried to swallow, but her throat felt as though it were filled with sawdust. Hot tears trickled down her cheeks as she embraced Mo. She couldn't imagine life without her. "Of course I'll take care of him," she answered in a hushed voice.

Andrea spent the next forty-eight hours in a blur of anguish. In addition, she listened to Mo browbeat herself for luring her to Phoenix and not delivering on the training she'd promised, and for deluging her instead with responsibilities, especially taking care of Christopher.

As it turned out, Andrea now received a crash course in running a restaurant that included familiarizing herself with the various recipes, delivery schedules and payroll. She followed Mo like a shadow, trying to absorb anything and everything that could help her resolve any problems that might arise in her absence. The exhausting schedule, coupled with her preoccupation with her friend, kept her stomach tied in a painful knot.

Besides worrying about Mo, Andrea fought to suppress the hollow yearning she felt every time Madison would creep into her mind. Impossible as it seemed, she admitted to herself that she missed him. Andrea Dusseaux, you fool! she admonished herself, reluctant to put into words what she feared to be true. How could she have allowed herself to fall in love with this man when there were so many negatives? She could never sacrifice her friendship with Mo. Besides, in a little over two weeks, or whenever Mo was recovered, she'd be back in New York.

But even as she strained to convince herself it would be best for everyone involved, she couldn't banish Madison from her thoughts. That night, collapsing into bed, a feverish dream tortured her, waking her with a start as the first faint light of dawn seeped through the blinds. She sat up and hugged the bedcovers around her trembling body as she relived every vivid detail.

He'd come into her darkened bedroom, pulled the sheet away from her naked body, then slid in beside her. She'd stiffened. He had no right to be here, she told him, but the words of protest died on her lips as he covered them with his. Her mind commanded her to resist, but instead she found herself yielding to the sensuous pleasure of having his gentle fingers trail over her body, caressing, exploring . . .

With ragged breath, she tossed aside the covers and rose to pull the blinds up and allow the morning light to fill the room, hoping it would dispel the torrid fantasies, extinguish the longing in her heart and body.

She managed to relegate Madison to the deepest recesses of her mind until Friday afternoon when she answered the phone in the restaurant's foyer. The shock of hearing his voice took her breath away.

"I hate to do this at the last minute, but I'm getting together with some friends for tennis after dinner. Our fourth canceled. Would you be interested?"

Her face was hot, her hands damp. "Well, I don't think s. . . ."

"It's not a date or anything," he interjected quickly. "Just tennis, nothing more. If you'd be more comfortable, I won't even pick you up. You can just meet us at the club."

His impartial tone bothered her, but, she reminded herself severely, she was the one who had taken what was probably just a friendly kiss and elevated it to such unrealistic heights. After all, they'd only known each other five days. She pressed a hand to her breast and hoped her voice didn't shake. "Thanks. Tennis sounds lovely, but I really can't." Keeping her voice cool, she explained briefly about Mo.

"I'm very sorry to hear this." He sounded genuinely concerned. "Please give her my best."

"I'll tell her. And thanks again for the tennis invite. Perhaps another time." She jumped when she felt Mo's hand on her shoulder and, from the agitated look on her face, realized she had probably overheard the entire conversation.

"Is that Madison?" Mo hissed, jabbing her finger at the receiver.

"Excuse me," Andrea told him, then covered the mouthpiece. "Yes, it is," she whispered." They need a fourth for doubles, and I've already said no."

Mo waved her hand impatiently. "Go. Go! It will do you good. After these last couple of days, you could use a breather."

In view of Mo's less-than-warm feelings for Madison, the suggestion astonished her. "Are you serious?"

"Completely. Besides, with me leaving in the morning, I could use some alone time with Christopher tonight." She gestured toward the phone. "Go on. Say yes."

Her eyes fixed on Mo, Andrea wrestled with her own tumultuous emotions. Wouldn't it be best if she didn't see him again? It took great effort to suppress the eager anticipation that filled her as she raised the phone to her ear. "Can you lend me a racket?"

Chapter Six

Despite Madison's earlier promise to himself that he could control his emotions and keep her at arm's length, his pulse skyrocketed as he watched Andrea walking toward him across the tennis court. He hoped the surge of longing to reach out, enfold her in his arms and kiss those sensuous lips didn't show on his face.

Dressed in a blue tennis shirt and matching skirt, her gait was elegant and seamless, as though she were floating. With great effort, he tore his gaze from her long slender legs and let it roam upwards, coming to rest on her heart-shaped face. Her beauty, coupled with her self-assured carriage, made his breath catch in his throat. He regretted, as he had a thousand times in the last two days, having accepted the Sundial House case. Suddenly, healing the long-standing rift between the Stantons and McKees didn't seem nearly as important. Reeling in Maureen Callaway could mean losing any chance he might have with Andrea.

Coming out of the clubhouse, Andrea spotted Madison on the tennis court standing near the net, flanked by a

young couple. She was so nervous it was all she could do
to keep from stumbling. How her legs managed to hold
her up, she didn't know. The distance seemed endless as
she approached them. The bright overhead lights emphasized the burnished copper color of his thick hair while
the perfect fit of his white shirt and tennis shorts accentuated his muscular physique and contrasted with his tan.
The vision of his naked body in last night's dream swam
before her. Disconcerted, she prayed her feelings wouldn't
betray her. It was a mistake to have come. Not in a million
years would she have accepted his invitation had Mo not
pressured her.

"I'm glad you could make it," he said as she came up
beside him.

"Thanks for inviting me."

Entranced by the gentle smile that lit his face and eyes,
Andrea was slow to react as he introduced her to his companions.

"This is Alan and Shirley Wilcox." He gestured in her
direction. "Andrea Dusseaux."

She shook hands with them, thinking that their identical
red hair, blue eyes and freckles made them look more like
brother and sister than a married couple.

After everyone praised the warm spring night, they
moved to a nearby bench where Madison extracted a racket
from his sports bag and extended it to her.

"If you're not comfortable with this one," he said, "we
can switch on the second game."

She recognized the top-of-the-line brand name.
"Thanks."

"I'm spinning for serve," Shirley announced, twirling
her racket. "Up or down?"

"Andrea, you choose," Madison suggested.

She won the serve and took her position behind the
baseline. In an attempt to overcome her preoccupation
with Madison, Andrea threw herself wholeheartedly into

the match. For the first time in days all the problems were swept aside as a feeling of well-being flooded her body. She'd forgotten what great therapy this all-encompassing game was.

Madison's appreciation for her grew as he watched her block the most difficult shots and easily outplay Shirley, who struggled to return her powerful crosscourt drive. When Andrea's final net shot won them the match, he was filled with awe. Not only was the woman a vision of grace and beauty, her game had been flawless.

"Thank you. This is a great racket," she said, handing it to him. "It made all the difference."

He gave her a sideways grin. "I don't think it was the racket."

"Yeah, Madison, dirty pool. I didn't know I'd be up against Martina Navratilova," Shirley teased, reaching across the net to give him a playful tap on the shoulder.

"I didn't either." His warm gaze on Andrea communicated his admiration.

Alan interjected loudly, "Hey, I can't accept this defeat. My ego is shattered. How about one more set?"

"I'm pooped," Shirley groaned, running a towel over her damp hair. "Why don't you guys play singles. I'll treat Andrea to iced cappuccino in the dining room. Join us when you're done."

Andrea tucked a strand of hair behind her ear as she cast a quick glance at Madison. The message in his eyes said, *It's up to you.*

She didn't trust herself in a social situation with him, but seeing the expectant look on Shirley's face, she decided it would seem rude to turn down the friendly offer. "An iced cappuccino sounds great." Even when the men joined them later, she would be on safe ground in a group situation.

The intimate atmosphere of the dining room, with the rich brocade wall paper and crystal light fixtures, briefly brought to mind the many hours she'd spent at the country club as a means to avoid going home to an empty house and waiting for Bernard. She sighed, grateful those sad days were behind her. As they sipped their coffee, Andrea could tell by the look in Shirley's eyes that the questions were coming.

Shirley steepled her fingers under her chin and smiled. "Alan and I go way back with Madison. Can we look forward to seeing the two of you together off the court, or is this strictly tennis?"

"Strictly tennis," Andrea replied, relieved that Shirley had handed her the perfect explanation. She would have been at a loss to describe her involvement with Madison. Come to think of it, maybe this *was* the truth as far as *he* was concerned. Throughout the evening he'd paid her no more attention than anyone else. And thinking back to the matter-of-fact tone when he'd called to invite her, not offering to pick her up—which she would have appreciated since she had a hard time finding the place—she was convinced that a tennis partner was absolutely all he had in mind.

"Too bad," Shirley said with a naughty wink. "He's a great catch."

"I'm sure he is." Andrea hoped the nonchalance in her voice would discourage any further discussion of Madison and quickly directed the conversation to Shirley who seemed only too happy to talk about herself for a while.

"Madison mentioned that you're visiting from New York. How much longer will you be here?"

"About two weeks."

"Well, I must be a glutton for punishment," she began with a gleam of amusement in her cornflower blue eyes, "but give me your telephone number in case I can get together a game or two before you leave."

Andrea scribbled the number on a napkin, then glanced at her watch. It was ten-thirty. Christopher was probably in bed by now, and with Mo on the threshhold of such a crucial step, she felt a desperate need to be with her.

"I didn't realize it was so late and I have to drive a friend to the airport in the morning. Would you mind if I left you alone?"

"It's fine by me," she answered with a shrug, "but I hope Madison won't be too disappointed."

Shirley's tone suggested she hadn't believed that tennis was the only connection between her and Madison. Andrea hoped that nothing in her own behavior betrayed the feelings she was so sure she'd kept under wraps.

"I think he'll understand. Please thank him for me and thanks for the cappuccino. I enjoyed meeting you."

She rose and left by the French doors that led to the parking lot. Half way toward her car something made her turn around in time to see Madison and Alan enter the dining room and join Shirley. She had just missed him.

"Good thing," she muttered under her breath, turning away. It had been difficult enough to pull off the Oscar-winning performance that conveyed she wasn't in love with this man, without putting herself through the agony of sitting in the same room with him for another hour.

With a heavy heart, she crossed to her car and withdrew the keys from her purse. She jumped when she heard Madison call out to her, then saw him running toward her. She tingled with elation.

Slightly out of breath, he came up beside her. "If you'd waited, I would have walked you to your car."

"I didn't know how long you'd be and I had to go." Whatever he said next, she didn't hear. She was too busy taking in the damp shirt that clung to his muscular torso. The sheen of perspiration on his skin made her want to touch it, to feel its heat. His close presence added fuel to the desire that overwhelmed her, leaving her knees weak, her pulse soaring. She glanced up at his face—a magnificent study of light and shadow—and fought down the urge to press her body against him, draw his lips down to crush hers.

She chided herself mentally, shocked at her aggressive sexual thoughts. It wasn't like her at all. She drew in a deep breath and donned the aloof mask she'd hidden behind for years. Madison would take the initiative, if he was still interested. Her heart hammered as they stood facing each other, but he made no move to touch her.

"I hope everything will be okay with Maureen."

She shook off her disappointment. "I hope so too."

There was an awkward moment of silence. "Great game. I'm glad you could make it."

"Me too." She got in and drove away, swallowing back the tears of frustration that stung her eyes.

It had been a foolish fantasy to imagine that his following her out into the parking lot entailed more than the mere courtesy of seeing a guest to the car. Her misinterpretation of his kiss that night left her feeling deflated. His desire to see her again must have been based on nothing more than pure physical attraction, otherwise, how could such a strong interest dissipate in just a few days? Obviously it had taken little effort on his part to turn a page and close the book on the whole thing.

Madison watched the taillights of her car vanish in the distance. It had taken all the willpower he possessed not to sweep her into his arms and tell her how much he cared for her. But her cold reserve had stopped him. He knew himself well enough to recognize that the strong physical attraction he'd had for her initially had grown into a deep emotional connection that surpassed by light-years anything he'd felt for anyone before.

He turned and walked back to the clubhouse, his blood singing in his ears. Why was she being so difficult? All he wanted to do was love her. He cursed the gods of fate that had prompted his father to place him in such an awkward position. Damn it! He wished he could allow himself to go back on his promise, take the heat and once and for all remove the obstacle that separated her from him. He paused near the doorway for a few minutes to regain his composure before rejoining his friends.

Andrea found Mo seated on the porch when she returned, an iced glass of lemonade in her hand. The bright moonlight made her face look pinched and bluish. Her heart contracted as the full impact of what was about to happen pierced her senses. Andrea sat down on the step at Mo's feet. The warm scent of jasmine from the garden seemed cloying tonight.

"Want some?" Mo asked, raising her drink. "I have a whole pitcher in the refrigerator."

"Thanks, I'm full of iced coffee."

"You sound down. Don't tell me you got beat in tennis?"

"No," she replied quietly.

Mo leaned her head against the back of the chair, staring upward. "I've been sitting here thinking. It's funny how you take your health for granted, then wham! Something happens and everything has a different perspective. Your priorities change. You open your eyes and take stock of what's around you, what's really important." She dropped her head forward and fixed her gaze on Andrea. "You know what I mean?"

"Yes. Divorce certainly isn't in the same league as your problem, but it forced me to take stock of my life. That's why I'm here."

"And am I glad you are. Speaking of putting things in perspective, I've changed my mind about letting Christopher go to Sedona."

Andrea's jaw dropped. "I don't believe it."

Mo hunched forward and laced her hands together. "I have a real blind spot when it comes to Sundial House but, on the flip side, I wasn't being fair to Christopher.

Lord knows I haven't been very good company these last few months and the kid is dying to get on a horse."

"Are you blaming yourself for being sick?"

"No. But I shouldn't be punishing him just because the person who invited him happens to be Madison McKee. I have a perfect opportunity to help him get his mind on something else besides me, and I almost blow it."

"Christopher's whining didn't have anything to do with this change of heart did it?"

Mo smiled and smacked her on the arm. "How did you guess?" She paused. "I have to consider your feelings too."

"What are you talking about?"

"Hey, this is your old buddy Mo, remember? Do you think I can't tell there's something's happening between you and Madison?"

"There's nothing happening."

"Of course not. That's why he called you up and asked you to play tennis."

"And that's all it was."

"I see. Well, in that case, your accompanying Christopher to Sedona should pose no threat."

"I don't even know if the invitation is still open."

"Oh no! I can't disappoint him now. I already told him he can go. I'm counting on you to call Madison tomorrow morning after you take me to the airport."

Andrea didn't know whether to laugh or cry. "I guess I could ask."

Mo smiled for the first time in days. "Thanks, kiddo. I hope I'm not putting you on the spot."

Andrea drew back in mock horror. "You? Put me on the spot? Heaven forbid!"

At the airport early the next morning, Andrea stood near the boarding gate, almost oblivious to the pandemonium around her, watching Mo kneel and press Christopher tightly against her. The farewell scene between mother and son made her throat constrict. Mo's pledge not to cry deserted her and she swiped hastily at the tears as Christopher drew back from the embrace.

"Don't cry, Mommy."

"Remember your promise not to give Andie a hard time."

Eyes wide, he solemnly crossed his heart. "I won't. I'll be very very good. And when you come back your headaches will be all gone, won't they?"

She pushed his glasses back up on the bridge of his nose. "You bet," she said with false bravado, while her soulful glance at Andrea communicated her inner doubts.

As the final page to board the plane sounded, Mo hugged Andrea. "Thanks, kiddo," she whispered, then taking her friend's hand, she joined it with Christopher's, held them tightly for a few seconds, then turned and disappeared into the ramp leading to the plane.

Andrea's repressed emotions suddenly surfaced as the symbolism of the gesture sunk in, bringing home the full ramifications of her responsibilites, should something happen to Mo. Her heart contracted painfully as she grasped the little boy's hand and led him back to the car.

On the drive out of the airport, Christopher waved frantically as a shrieking jet rose overhead. "I'll bet that's Mommy's plane." He craned his head to watch until it was out of sight, then turned to Andrea. "Are we gonna call Madison now?"

While she concentrated on merging into freeway traffic, she marveled at children's ability to block out trouble and replace it with happier thoughts. "As soon as we get home, honey."

She would have preferred to delay the awkward chore a little longer, reluctant to reopen communication with Madison after his impersonal treatment of her the night before. Unfortunately she did not enjoy the luxury of putting off the call, for no sooner had she opened the front door than Christopher raced to the phone and extended the receiver to her. "Call Madison. Call Madison!" he shouted, jumping up and down, his eyes shining with anticipation.

With strong misgivings, she looked up Madison's number and dialed, half hoping he wouldn't be home.

"Hello." The sound of his deep resonant voice left her tongue-tied. How should she begin?

"It's Andrea." She paused for a second, then quickly jumped in before she lost her nerve. "Is that invitation to Sedona still open?" Without waiting for his reply, she added hastily, "Of course, if you've made other plans, I'll understand." The stretch of silence that followed her question made her feel small.

"Yeah, it's open."

She thought she detected a lack of enthusiasm in his voice.

"What time is it?"

She glanced at her watch and, to her horror, realized it was barely seven-thirty. Her stomach fluttered with embarrassment. "Oh, no. I woke you. We've been up so long, I didn't realize it was still an uncivilized hour."

"I'm happy to hear from you anytime. But tell me, where did this change of heart come from all of a sudden?"

Before she could answer, Christopher pulled on her arm. "Let me talk to him!"

"Here's Christopher."

He was pink with excitement as she handed him the receiver. "My mommy says I can go! My mommy says I can go!" He listened wide-eyed to whatever Madison said to him and then shoved the phone back to Andrea. "Whoopee!"

Amused, Andrea watched him cavort around the room as she put the receiver to her ear. "Somehow I think he's just a teeny bit excited."

Madison laughed. "Well, I'm looking forward to it too." His tone serious now, he added, "And I hope you're looking forward to coming as well."

Her pulse rate escalated, but she kept her voice casual. "I'm sure it will be fun."

"I'll pick you both up at eight, if that's not too early."

"I doubt it. If Christopher sleeps a wink tonight I'll be surprised."

The following morning when they reached Sedona, Madison pulled the Range Rover off the narrow, winding road and stopped on the crest of a hill. He gestured out the windshield. "Well, what do you think?"

Andrea's gaze swept over the tree-filled valley and moved upward to the jagged formations of vermilion-colored rocks that spired into the cobalt-blue sky. Puffy white clouds cast irregular shadows that draped the cliffs like black sheets. Enthralled, she clapped her hands together. "Ohhh! I've never seen anything like it in my life!"

She turned to Madison and caught him watching her. Held captive by the bold message burning in his eyes, she felt the blood rush to her cheeks. Once again, his compelling presence penetrated her defenses and left her feeling giddy and vulnerable. She averted her eyes, afraid to admit the strong feelings she had for this man. Feelings that heightened with each moment. Feelings that brought pangs of guilt as she thought of Mo.

"Alters to the gods, some say," Madison said softly, thinking that nature had not only bestowed exceptional beauty on the surrounding scenery, but on this enchanting woman as well. She looked wonderful. No, luscious. Her black headband made a striking contrast to her light blonde hair, while the matching pullover hugged the sensuous swell of her breasts, then tapered down to the delicate waist. Snug tan jeans accentuated her shapely thighs. His desire for her was overwhelming. He longed to pull her to him, caress her, kiss away the last shadows of distrust that always seemed to lurk behind her wary blue eyes.

Acutely aware of his continuing scrutiny, Andrea was thankful when Christopher's question from the back seat broke the silence.

"When do we get to ride the horses, Madison?" The coloring book, crayons and puzzles had kept him busy for most of the two hour trip, but she recognized the restless tone in his voice.

"We're on our way." Madison shifted into gear and steered onto the highway.

On the drive through the downtown area, she was only half paying attention as Madison pointed out quaint shops and million dollar homes nestled in the crimson hills.

She sneaked a sideways glance at him. The man was every bit as handsome in jeans and boots as in an expensive business suit. Her eyes lingered on the fringe of curly chestnut hair the open collar of his checkered shirt revealed. She folded her hands tightly in her lap as though curbing the temptation to touch him.

She'd been surprised by his warm demeanor when he'd picked them up earlier, and more than pleased by his concern when he urged her to bring along jackets for her and Christopher in case of a sudden change in the weather. He'd inquired about Mo's condition and comforted her with words of optimism. In fact, he was attentive during the entire ride with not a trace of his impersonal behavior from Friday night. Had she imagined the whole thing?

As she sorted out her jumbled feelings, she knew there was no use denying it. She was in love with this man and wanted him more than anything she'd ever wanted in her life. Yet coming to grips with her inner emotions gave her no peace of mind. The conflict surrounding Mo's property was as ominous as storm clouds.

Madison turned onto a bumpy dirt road and carefully

maneuvered the vehicle over the bare rocks, to make the ride as gentle as possible for Andrea while Christopher, giggling with delight, urged him to go fast so he could bounce higher. The road widened into a gravelled clearing and a single-story stone ranchhouse, surrounded by giant green tamarisk trees, came into view.

Madison pulled up beside his sister Miriam's red pickup truck and got out. He stretched and drew in breaths of the mesquite-tinged air. He loved the ranch and always looked forward to visiting. Even though six years separated them, he had always felt closer to Miriam than to his brother, Michael, who was only two years his senior.

He opened the back door, unbuckled Christopher's seatbelt and swung him into the air before lowering him to the ground.

"Wow!" Christopher shouted, stamping his feet to raise puffs of coral dust. "It looks like somebody painted the dirt red!"

Madison exchanged an amused glance with Andrea. "It's the sandstone the wind blew off the rocks." They turned toward the house as a screen door flew open.

"Well, it's about time you city folk got here!" Miriam announced with mock severity.

Dressed in a blue western shirt, long denim skirt and boots, she strode toward them across the driveway, trying to sidestep the two frisky Labradors that bounded out the door with her.

Madison couldn't help but notice how much she resembled their mother, whose once rich brown hair had also turned prematurely white by her late thirties.

"Settle down, you guys," Miriam admonished the dogs as she reached to restrain each by the collar.

Andrea didn't miss the appraising gleam in the woman's brown eyes.

"Madison told me on the phone you were a real knockout and he sure didn't exaggerate," Miriam said, throwing a broad wink in his direction, while giving Andrea a sturdy handshake.

"Thank you." Andrea tapped the dust from her shoes to hide her delight and embarrassment. She was surprised that he'd volunteered such information to his sister and wondered what else he'd told her.

"So you're the little lad who wants to be a cowpoke," Miriam said, turning her attention to Christopher. He nodded shyly. "Have you ever ridden before?"

"A pony, but not a real horse."

Miriam's eyes sparkled. "Well, we're gonna fix that right now. Tell you what, you can all come in, freshen up, and then," she said placing a hand on Christopher's shoulder, "my foreman will let you pick out whatever horse your little heart desires."

An hour later, Christopher proudly sat astride the black quarterhorse he'd chosen, while Madison led him around the corral explaining how to handle the reins.

"The boy's got natural ability," Miriam remarked to Andrea as they both stood outside the fence, watching. "Plus that, my brother's always had a real knack for relating to kids."

"He's certainly a hit with Christopher."

"You know, it's a real shame. If it hadn't been for that fiasco, he'd probably have one or two of his own by now."

"You mean him breaking off his engagement?"

"Ha!" She threw her head back derisively. "I can't believe he told you that. He knows darn well that was purely for public consumption."

"Well, actually he didn't say much about it at all." Andrea was puzzled. She wanted to know more, but didn't wish to appear overly anxious. "Madison was telling us about your boys on the way up here. Sounds like you had your hands full with twins."

A wistful smile lit her face. "They kept me on my toes, but I wouldn't have traded it for anything. It was a real kick in the pants to have them both go off to college at the same time." At that moment the ranch foreman rode up and asked if she wanted the other horses saddled. "Let's hold off on that till after lunch, Gus." Miriam turned back to Andrea. "I just have a light meal planned for now because we're having a big barbeque for dinner."

Later during lunch, Miriam suggested that they might all enjoy watching cattle being branded on the south range. Christopher whooped his approval.

Madison noticed the faint look of repugnance that crossed Andrea's face. He quickly suggested that perhaps she might prefer to join him instead on a horseback ride to what he described as one of the most beautiful spots in the state.

Glad to be rescued from having to witness the branding, Andrea cast him a grateful look, but hesitated, saying that she should probably stay with Christopher.

Miriam waved away her protest. "You two go on by yourselves and have a good time. This little cowboy will be fine with me."

Andrea felt a delicious heat flow through her as she met the gleam of pleasure in Madison's eyes. The unexpected opportunity to spend the afternoon alone with him was a tantalizing prospect indeed.

Chapter Seven

Andrea sighed contentedly and raised her face to the patches of warm afternoon sun filtering through the wispy branches of the sycamore trees. A breeze rippled through the canopy of leaves and mingled with the soft clip-clop of the horses' hooves on the sandy path. Other than the occasional call of a bird, those were the only sounds that disturbed the hush of the canyon. Yet she knew the sensation of euphoria gripping her had very little to do with the breathtaking scenery, and everything to do with the man riding beside her.

Madison let his gaze sweep over her as he'd done a dozen times since they'd left the ranch a half hour earlier. When she turned her head and settled those magnificent eyes on him, a sweet ache filled his heart. The opportunity to be alone with her was an unexpected gift and he intended to make the most of it. He heard her sigh again.

"Are you getting tired?"

"Not a bit. I had a pony when I was a kid and rode every

chance I got." She smiled. "Why? How much further is your favorite lookout point?"

"We cross the creek, and then it's another hour's climb to the top of that ridge."

She looked in the direction he indicated and flashed him another brilliant smile. "From the way you described it, I can hardly wait to get there."

He was overwhelmed with a heady mixture of tenderness and desire. The possibility that her feelings for him might be as strong as his for her sent a current of excitement through him.

As they approached the wooden bridge spanning the swift-running creek, he reined in his horse. The water level seemed much higher than usual.

She noticed his frown. "Is this safe?" she asked tentatively.

"I'm sure it's fine. We had a good snowpack this past winter. It's just normal runoff." He shook off the twinge of uneasiness as he crossed the bridge and glanced up at the cloudless sky. Marion had mentioned at lunch that a storm was forecast, but wasn't expected until tomorrow.

"Come on, Abigail," Andrea said, spurring her horse and keeping it close behind his as hooves splashed in the water flowing over the planks. She noticed that he repeatedly turned to watch her and was touched by his concern. He was like a parent watching over a child's first steps.

She masked her nervousness as the horses left the canyon floor and began the laborious ascent up the mountain. Noting it was steeper than she had expected, she gave one apprehensive glance behind her, then forced herself to look straight ahead. She was eager to see the calendar-picture view he had depicted. But it was the chance to be alone with him that made her stomach flutter with anticipation.

A sudden gust of cold wind startled Madison. It whistled

eerily through the pines, causing his horse to stop on the rocky, cactus-strewn trail and let out a nervous whinny.

"What's wrong?" she asked in a tense voice.

He patted his animal's lathered neck. "I think the wind scared him."

He didn't like the mass of clouds that had suddenly appeared overhead, but threw Andrea an encouraging smile, while he fumed inwardly. He knew damned good and well how quickly the weather could change this time of year and he should have been paying closer attention. The swollen creek had provided the first clue that something wasn't right and he'd selfishly chosen to ignore it. If it was already raining in the mountains to the north they might be in trouble. He urged his horse upward. He'd have a clear view of the valley from the crest of the hill.

Andrea drew in an appreciative breath when they rode out above the tree line and reined in the horses at the summit that overlooked the stark beauty of the jagged red rocks rising from the ravine below. "This is absolutely magnificent! It's like standing on top of the world."

In one graceful movement he dismounted and moved to help her down, reaching up to encircle her waist as she swung her leg over. She placed her hands on his shoulders and a delicious shiver chased through her as she slid to the ground in front of him. His fingers lingered on her hips and suddenly all the reservations she'd felt toward him vanished. The passion blazing in his eyes ignited her senses.

"Thank you for bringing me to this magical place," she whispered.

"Magical is a good way to describe it now that you're here."

It was only a split-second hesitation before she went into his arms, willingly, his warm lips on hers sending chills zigzagging up and down her spine. She parted her lips, losing all sense of time and place as she allowed his tongue to roam and savor. Crushed against his lean body, she could feel the urgency of his passion growing.

She heard a faint rumble in the distance and he released her with a groan. The look of apprehension on his face sent a surge of confusion through her.

"We've got to go now. Quickly." The rough edge in his tone surprised her.

"Why?" she asked breathlessly, her head still reeling from the spell of their embrace.

"Because of that." He spun her around to confront the bank of clouds boiling on the horizon. Angry thunderheads hung over the distant peaks. "Looks like we're in for more than a spring shower." He gave her a leg up into the saddle. "We'd better get back down to the bridge fast. That heavy rain in the mountains could soon make it impossible for us to cross." He swung onto his horse, spurring it down the hill.

He'd tried to keep his voice light, not wanting to panic her. Damn, he should have checked the weather forecast again before leaving. His stomach clenched as he turned and saw the clouds rolling towards them like black waves in the quickening wind. If they didn't get back across the bridge in a hurry, they might be stranded in the forest.

Alarmed at the force of the wind, Andrea tucked in her arms and grabbed the pommel hard. "It looks like a tornado! Are we going to make it back to the ranch before it hits?"

"We'll certainly give it a try."

She prayed the animals were sure-footed and leaned back against the downward rush, afraid she might tumble off. "I hope you know what you're doing, Abigail," she muttered under her breath, thankful that Christopher was safe with Marion.

She regretted that the glorious moment had been so abruptly shattered, their delicious togetherness transformed into a tumultous downhill charge. She followed his lead, her heartbeat matching the pounding of the horses' hooves.

She caught up with him as he reached the bridge, just as his horse reared and let out a startled whinny. He grabbed her reins to steady her mount as she pulled abreast of him. Her pulse speeding at the sight of the bridge buried under the churning water, she looked at Madison for assurance.

He shook his head in stunned disbelief as he watched the water roiling over the planks, inundating them. "We're too late," he shouted over the churning creek and the scream of the wind.

"Is there another way to cross?"

He heard the fright in her voice. "Yes, but it's five miles from here!"

He looked around searching for another solution, knowing full well there was none. The only thing he could think of was to seek help at the fire tower up the mountain, which meant they'd be riding into the teeth of the storm. The bright flash of lightning, followed by an ear splitting crack of thunder, made up his mind quickly.

"There's a forest service road over there. We'll head for the fire tower." He wheeled his horse around. "Can you make it?"

Realizing it was more a statement than a question, Andrea gave a wordless nod and put her trust in Madison, wishing she were with him on his horse, pressed close, drawing comfort from his strength.

She heard the rustle of rain rushing through the trees seconds before she felt it on her face. Her fingers stiffened as the temperature plunged and wind tore at her hair and clothing. She hung onto Abigail's neck with a fierceness she didn't know she possessed. A branch bent by Madison's horse ahead of her whipped back, stinging her cheek. She winced with pain, but consoled herself with the thought that soon they would be in a warm safe place.

Madison prodded his horse into a lope when they reached the dirt road. He kept glancing over his shoulder to see if Andrea was all right. Fury and guilt tortured him. The notion that he was responsible if anything happened to her, sickened him.

Several felled pines lay across the road, slowing their arduous journey and, after what seemed an interminable length of time, he squinted ahead and saw the black skeleton of the fire tower looming through the mist. Relief was replaced by uncertainty when he noticed no welcoming lights. His heart sank as they drew nearer. There was no forest service truck parked at the base, no sign of life, nothing. Madison cursed under his breath as he remembered the old tower was being abandoned for a new one erected two miles further east on a higher ridge. He hadn't realized that the move had been completed.

He jumped off his horse and ran to help Andrea. Her knees gave way and she almost tumbled to the ground, but he caught her and held her quaking body to him. If he had to break down the door to get in, he'd do it.

Madison gestured to the stairs spiraling up into the low-hanging clouds that swirled overhead. "Hope you're not afraid of heights."

Andrea shook her head. "I'll be fine."

Under ordinary circumstances the climb would have been exhilarating, but ascending into the belly of a violent storm made her heart stumble. She waited in silent misery while he tethered the horses before turning and grasping her hand in his. Together, they scaled the stairs, fighting for balance as the ferocious wind assaulted them.

Halfway up, they were pelted with hail that made a deafening clatter against the metal steps. Her teeth chattered so hard she was afraid they would crack. They reached the landing, gasping for breath.

Madison prepared to shoulder the door open and felt a jolt of surprise when the handle turned easily. Without bothering to analyze why it had been left unlocked, he flung the door aside, pulled Andrea in and slammed it shut behind them. After enduring so much time in the storm, it seemed eerily quiet in the blessedly-dry room. Outside, lightning flashed with fury, but the roar of rain and thunder was muted.

He felt along the wall for a light switch, hoping the power was still on. It wasn't. His spirits sank. He hadn't seen an emergency generator down below either. He squinted into the darkened space. Most everything was gone, including the telescope and radio.

He wished he could contact Marion. She'd be worried and had probably called the sheriff's department by now— for whatever good that would do, he thought, remembering all the debris that blocked the road.

Disappointment left him hollow as he continued looking around. All that remained was the bare kitchen counter, a built-in table and bed. A flannel shirt hung in an otherwise empty closet. He was thankful for the pile of logs and newspapers in the corner. At least the old wood stove offered some measure of hope.

He turned to Andrea, who stood shivering in the middle of the room, water dripping from her hair and clothing forming a puddle on the floor. "There's no light or radio, but at least we can start a fire. I've got matches in my saddlebag, so I'll ..." He paused, hearing her sneeze. "Those wet clothes have to come off." He suppressed his amusement at the look of horror on her face. "Take this." He grabbed the shirt from the closet and pressed it into her icy hands before opening the door to the driving rain.

Andrea decided it must be her light-headedness that made her think the pounding water sounded like applause at a Broadway show. She'd witnessed many a storm, but had never in her life experienced anything quite like this one.

She wanted to change quickly before he returned, but

her stiff fingers made the removal of her clothes a monu-
mental task. She shuddered with relief when she wrapped
the dry flannel around her naked body and made her way
to the edge of the bed, her rubbery legs barely able to
support her. She sat hugging her knees to her chest, her
feet tucked underneath the huge shirt, and cocooned herself into a tight ball until her shivering subsided.

She heard his footsteps and braced herself against the
cold wind that rushed in with him. He kicked the door
shut and dropped the saddle bags at his feet. "Damn, it's
cold!"

Her eyes now accustomed to the gloom, Andrea watched
as he crumpled newspaper, then jumbled wood into the
stove. With the scrape of the match, welcome golden light
filled the room along with the sharp odor of sulphur. She
felt herself go limp with relief at the glorious sight of the
crackling blaze. With one strong tug, Madison unsnapped
and stripped off his wet shirt, laying it flat beside the stove.

He rubbed his hands vigorously and blew into them.
"This place will warm up soon." He knelt to add another
log, using the poker to coax the orange tongues of flame
to life.

Mesmerized by the sight of his taut muscles highlighted
by the fire, moving like steel underneath the glowing skin,
she forgot her own discomfort. She studied the outline of
his narrow hips, powerful thighs, and she was gripped by
a raw primal urge deep within her, compelling her to throw
aside all logic, all inhibitions, all reason. She rose and
gravitated toward him with only one thought driving her—
to touch him. She wanted this man, needed him, craved
him.

Madison laid the poker down, slid the fire screen in
place and stood studying the flames, aware that Andrea
had come up beside him. "That should do it." His heart
quickened when he turned and feasted his eyes on the
enchanting vision. There she stood, looking so fragile

wrapped in the huge shirt, her blue eyes wide, damp tendrils of golden hair spiraling down her pale cheeks.

His eyes dropped instinctively to her bare thighs and he turned away, disconcerted by the hardness manifesting itself in his groin. How could he entertain such thoughts when his misguided judgment had gotten her within an inch of her life? He should have taken better care of her. But the thought that she was naked underneath the shirt sent his pulse soaring so high that he struggled to control his labored breathing.

He self-consciously cleared his throat and held his hands out to the fire. "I'm sorry as hell I got you into this mess."

"I'm not." Her voice was low and husky.

Startled, he swung around and saw the simmering invitation in her eyes.

She slowly opened the shirt and spread it wide. "There's enough room in here for both of us."

The buttery glow of the flames played over her body as his hungry gaze took in her full round breasts, traveled over her flat belly to the gentle curve of her hips, and settled on the downy vee between her legs.

He couldn't believe it. Was this the unapproachable woman he'd been afraid to offend, suppressing his ardor, weighing his words, being careful with every move? She had seemed unattainable only hours earlier. He would have thought that this was the wrong time, the wrong place, and yet . . . everything felt superbly right. Hypnotized by the passion in her eyes, he closed the distance between them.

Tenderly, he cradled her face in his palms and looked deep into her eyes. "Are you sure?"

She reached up and took his hands, sliding them around her waist. Her velvety skin sent an electrifying shudder through him. "I've never been so sure of anything in my whole life."

She stood still, seeming not to breathe at all as he

touched his lips to her forehead, moved down to the tip of her nose and then with a groan, his mouth captured hers. His hands were on their own delightful journey, sliding down her back, coming to rest on her firm shapely bottom.

Andrea wrapped the shirt around him and pressed him to her, her mouth hungrily savoring his, now more urgent, more demanding, as unrestrained as the driving rain outside. She brushed her breasts against him, her nipples tense, luxuriating in the crisp hair on his powerful chest.

She was astonished at how readily she cast aside the years of inhibition, of reserve. She felt like a creature of nature, shedding its protective skin to welcome the advent of spring, to welcome life. The intensity of emotions building inside her bewildered her, as the mingling sensations of love and passion sent her mind spinning out of control, catapulting her into uncharted territory.

The spell was interrupted by the earthly impact of his cold wet blue jeans. Reluctantly she drew back and looked up at him. "These will have to come off," she purred, her fingers tugging at his belt buckle. Oh, my God! Is this really me? she thought, shocked by her boldness.

Madison reveled in the full permission that glowed in her eyes. "So does this," he whispered as he peeled away her shirt. He hesitated for a moment, awed by her sleek sensuous curves, then effortlessly swept her into his arms and carried her to the bed. His breath caught in his throat. He'd never been so ready to take a woman before. He pulled off his boots and stripped, all the while his eyes fixed on her face, yearning, expectant.

"My darling, darling, Andrea, you are without question the most beautiful woman I have ever seen."

The wild beating of her heart as she drank in his splendid nakedness pounded in her ears. The flickering shadows cast by the fire accentuated the taut muscles of his body and the rigid evidence of his desire. He stretched out beside her, and she let out a gasp of pleasure as his fingers gently circled one nipple, then moved to caress the other. A cold shiver along with a flash of heat prickled her skin as he traced a slow tantalizing path to her navel and down to her inner thighs, where he stroked, barely touching, teasing, sharpening her nerve endings, until she moaned aloud.

Lightning illuminated the room, allowing her to read the passion reflected in his dark eyes. She reached up and curled her fingers in his hair, pulling his face down to hers, opening her mouth to eagerly receive his kiss, urgent, hot, exploring. She answered his questing tongue with hungry probing of her own.

She arched toward him, aching for him to touch her where the core of her need throbbed. Disappointed for a moment when his fingers abandoned her thighs, her delight returned full force as he now fondled her breasts, cupping, stroking, his open palms coaxing her nipples to taut peaks, sharpening her excitement with each caress, driving her mad. He caught her lower lip in his teeth and gently nibbled, then once more fastened his lips firmly over hers.

She felt herself slipping away, yielding to sensations that were totally new to her, feelings that had simmered for so many years beneath the surface, emotions she had no yearning to understand or justify. With a sigh, she succumbed to the quickening inside her, blazing through every inch of her body.

Madison planted a final searing kiss to her lips, then sought her breasts, sucking first one straining nipple and then the other, syphoning her desire into a fever pitch. Andrea tingled as his warm mouth moved slowly down, lingered on her stomach, tasted her navel, then moved lower, lower, leaving her skin burning in the wake of his ardent kisses. She drew in a sharp breath when his lips touched the tender skin in the crease of her thighs, her innermost core pulsating, expectant, as she shifted her body, allowing him full access.

Madison felt a sweet ache as he savored the satin-smoothness of her inner thighs, breathed in the scent of her skin, heady as incense. Her supple body undulated under him, gathering him closer, inciting his arousal, filling him with an unbearably delicious agony. He felt her tense, heard her surprised gasp at the first deliberate touch of his tongue as he tasted her. She moaned softly as his tongue slipped into her sweet, wet depths, as he drank in her nectar. He struggled to maintain control of his own growing passion as she repeatedly uttered his name, the pleading in her voice inflaming his senses, taking him to the edge.

He raised his body over her. "Oh, Andrea, Andrea," he groaned, seeking her ultimate consent. She parted her legs and he lowered himself into her.

All the ties that had held her in emotional bondage fell away as he embedded himself deep inside her, taking her with him with every fiber of her being. She clung to him, drawing him in deeper, knowing that she would never be the same again, that this culmination of their love made her feel complete, whole. No longer were there any fears keeping them apart or secrets separating them. She was moving with him now in a magnificent ancient ritual, taking him where there was no getting closer.

His breathing was erratic, hoarse. She clung to him in a wild frenzy, the roar of her own pounding heart effacing nature's tantrum outside, wiping away everything except the sweet aching sensation of their bodies flowing into one another. She squeezed her eyes shut as the tension inside her rose and a ragged cry tore from her throat as he brought her to the pinnacle of pleasure, every cell in her body vibrating as she reached the shattering crescendo.

She exhaled a long, shuddery breath as the sensation slowly ebbed, leaving her with the disquieting thought that the old Andrea Dusseaux no longer existed. The last vestiges of the fortress she'd built around her emotions had crumbled away, leaving her unshackled, superbly free.

When she opened her eyes and met his, another thrill raced through her. The gleam in his gaze expressed triumph and elation in the knowledge that he had successfully brought her to the peak of ecstasy. Then his lips crushed hers again as he abandoned all pretense of holding back.

Exquisitely satiated, she indulged herself in his accelerated thrusts, greedily relishing them as he climbed higher and higher. He shifted his weight suddenly, moving his hands underneath to cup her buttocks. His cry mingled with a crash of thunder and she felt a rash of goosebumps erupt on his skin as the explosion shuddered through him, signaling his release.

She held him tightly as he lay still, his ragged breathing gradually returning to normal. Her desire quenched, she floated in a gauzy cloud of contentment and dreamily watched the shadows from the flames dance on the ceiling. A ripple of amazement ran through her as she thought about what had just happened between them.

The room was lighter now as the storm abated. Rain still pattered on the windows, but the lightning was sporadic, the thunder a muted rumble in the distance. The possibility of spending the entire night here with Madison filled her with sublime warmth.

Madison reluctantly returned to earth when a log gave a loud pop and the fire flared, hissing and crackling. He planted a series of kisses on Andrea's neck, cheeks and lips before sliding his weight off her.

The sudden loss of his warm skin, coupled with the sheen of perspiration that had glued their bodies together, made Andrea shiver.

"You're cold," he said, pulling her firmly against him and massaging her skin.

"I love you, Andrea," he whispered. The words could not adequately describe the wealth of emotions that engulfed him. Surprised by the depth of his feelings for her, he swallowed hard, barely trusting himself to speak. "You may find this difficult to believe," he said, smoothing the tangle of curls from her face, "but I feel as if this is the first time I ever really made love."

Andrea's throat tightened in response as she saw his eyes brim with tenderness. He'd voiced the very words that she'd thought to herself, that she longed to say back to him. But could she? Did she dare trust her love to this man?

Madison caught the haunted expression that darkened her eyes before she turned her head away. It was the same unfathomable look she'd given him that first day. He slid a finger under her chin and drew her face back to him. "Why did you look at me like that?" When he saw her lips tremble he tightened his grip on her shoulder. "Who could have hurt you so much?"

She said nothing, simply looked at him with eyes huge with tears.

"Please tell me. I *need* you to tell me," he said in a low gutteral tone, "because I want to kiss away the hurt and love away all your pain."

Rapunsel rescued by the fair prince Andrea thought as her tears overflowed. "Oh, Madison, I wish I could, but I haven't talked about this with anyone. It's too painful."

He gently brushed away her tears and took her face in both hands, showering it with soft kisses. "Tell me."

She combed her fingers through her hair. "Oh, God, it's such a long story." She gave an involuntary shudder.

"I've got all night, but let me do one thing first."

She watched him quickly move to the stove, throw in another log, then gather up the flannel shirt and return to lay beside her, draping the shirt over them both. He propped himself up on one elbow and pressed her to him. His face glowed with a sweet boyish smile. "I'm all ears."

Andrea smiled back and, lifting her face, gave him a gentle kiss. She took a big breath and bared her soul to him, beginning with the loss of her mother to suicide when she was eight, her grandmother's death a year later, and her father's during her senior year in college. And finally the desolation in her marriage to Bernard, the irony of him depriving her of the child she longed for while leaving her for another woman who was having his baby. In spite of the pain of reliving it all, she felt a heady relief as though an onerous weight had been lifted from her, liberating her.

Madison tenderly traced her face with his fingertips when she'd finished. "Well, I'm certain of one thing," he said, stroking her hair.

"What?"

"Bernard must be the biggest idiot to ever walk the face of the earth."

She smiled ruefully. "No, I am. For transferring all my fears unfairly onto you."

"That's all behind us now."

"Can you now understand why it's so hard for me . . ."

"To trust any man?" Madison interjected.

She nodded silently.

His gaze bored into hers. "I'm not Bernard. You'll have to trust me, Andrea Dusseaux, because like it or not, I'm here to stay, to love you. What do you think of that?"

Andrea's heart was so full she could hardly speak. She swallowed a lump in her throat. "I think," she said, wrapping her arms around him, "that I love you very much, Madison McKee."

Chapter Eight

Eyes closed, Andrea stretched languidly, feeling faint surprise that she'd fallen asleep. Recollections of Madison's exquisite lovemaking gave her a sense of peace and happiness she'd never known before. Reaching for him, she felt an aching bewilderment when she realized he wasn't beside her, wasn't even in the room.

She sat up with a start and saw that his clothes and boots were gone. Hugging the flannel shirt to her breast, she swung her legs over the edge of the bed. She wondered how long she'd slept. The fire in the stove was low and she shivered as cool air met her bare back and shoulders. Brilliant flashes of lightning piercing the night sky told her the storm had not yet abated.

Where could he have gone? she wondered, padding across the cold floor to kneel in front of the stove. As thunder vibrated the windows a sudden thought struck her. Mo's surgery was scheduled for tomorrow morning and she'd promised to call tonight! She felt sick with guilt. As if Mo didn't have enough worries on her mind. A good thing she'd given her Marion's phone number so she could call and check on Christopher. Andrea prayed he was coping with the situation. She half smiled to herself as she thought of the little devil. He was probably having the time of his life at the ranch.

Another rumble of thunder shook the tower and she felt a ripple of uneasiness, wondering where Madison had disappeared to. The sound of his steps on the metal staircase outside brought a sigh of relief to her lips. The dying fire in the stove flared as he edged the door open as a gust of wind, thick with the of scent of rain and pines, swept into the room with him.

At the sight of her, Madison felt a surge of love and fierce protectiveness. She looked incredibly seductive swathed in the big checkered shirt, her eyes still smokey from slumber, her hair a tangled mass of gold.

"Well, sleepy-head, it's about time." He quickly shut the door and blew into his hands to warm them before he knelt and slipped an arm around her shoulders.

She gave him a coy glance. "I don't know how I could have fallen asleep."

He smiled. "Guess you exerted more energy than you bargained for."

"You mean the horseback riding?" she asked, mischief gleaming in her blue eyes.

His smile grew wicked. "That too."

"Where were you just now?"

"Checking on the horses, and I was kinda hoping there might be some dry wood stacked underneath the tower but I guess these last two logs will have to do for the night. If the fire goes out, I'll do my best to keep you warm," he said, sliding his arm down around her waist.

Andrea let him draw her to him and hold her tightly against his chest. In the lull between the cracks of thunder it was so quiet in the room, she could hear her heart drumming in her ears.

"Comfy?" he whispered, stroking her back.

"Yes," she sighed. "There's just one little thing."

He pulled back to look at her face. "What?"

"This will probably sound crazy but I'm starving."

He threw his head back laughing. "That barbeque dinner we were supposed to eat has crossed my mind once or twice too." He closed his eyes. "I can picture it now, a great big juicy steak, mouth-watering cowboy beans, buttermilk buisquits . . ."

She slapped his shoulder playfully. "Stop! That's cruel."

He gave her a teasing grin then reached for the saddlebag. "I always knew my Boy Scout training would come in handy someday. "How does water, apples and a chocolate bar sound?"

"Heavenly!"

"Let's make this easier on your beautiful bottom," he said, pushing to his feet and hauling the mattress near the fire.

She watched him set out the rations and slice the apples with a pocket knife. "Hmmm. Impromptu picnics seem to be your specialty. Strangely reminiscent of your pizza and paté." Andrea narrowed her eyes with mock accusation. "How many women besides me have you lured into this tower?"

"Dozens." He kept a straight face while his eyes blazed with mirth as he fed her a piece of apple. Suddenly serious, he reached out and gently stroked her cheek. "I want you to know that from this moment forward, you are the only one in my life."

Her heart sang as he voiced what she herself felt about him. She couldn't imagine ever loving another man. Studying him in the flickering light, she savored the memory of his lips on hers, his sensuous touch, his tender words of love. But what did she really know about him?

"Your sister said something rather provocative this morning—about your broken engagement being strictly for public consumption?'' she asked, looking at him expectantly.

He sighed with frustration. "Marion told you that?"

She drew back at his wary expression. "Have I hit on a taboo subject?"

"I wouldn't exactly call it that, but it's not something I'd planned to go into now."

Placing her hands on her hips, Andrea hunched her shoulders forward. "Oh, I see we have a double standard here. What's good for the goose isn't good for the gander."

"Touché." He absently stoked the fire. "Remember what I told you about the family rift? I guess I'd better give you a little background so you'll understand."

She folded her arms across her breast. "Go ahead. I'm not going anywhere."

"To everyone else in town she's the very refined Victoria Stanton, anchor woman, local celebrity and all that. But to me she's just the Vicky I grew up with. She was a really neat kid, sort of a tomboy and we were inseparable. As we got older, our parents made no secret of the fact that they hoped we'd end up together." He gave her a sheepish glance. "It was like a pre-ordained destiny, if you know what I mean."

"And somewhere along the way the camaraderie changed to love?" she said, raising a quizzical brow.

"Not for quite a while. I went to Harvard, she went to Carnegie Mellon in Pittsburgh. We dated other people, saw each other back and forth . . ."

"Dated? No meaningful relationships?"

"Yes, when I apprenticed with the law firm in Boston. But there was always something missing."

"And where was Victoria all this time?"

"She majored in broadcasting and got on at a TV station in Pittsburgh. So for a couple of years there, except for holidays and family gatherings, we didn't see too much of each other until we both ended up back in Phoenix."

"So you automatically gravitated back to Victoria."

"With a couple of fizzled relationships on each side, we figured if we weren't finding the right thing with someone else, then maybe this was the right thing—not to mention our parents getting into the act and tightening the screws on us to get married."

"And how did you get to be the bad guy?"

"Picture this," Madison sighed, ruffling his hair. "Russell throws us a lavish engagement party that hits all the society pages. Then while the wedding preparations are going on, he surprises the hell out of us by buying us a million dollar house, and the money to furnish it on top of that. It was like a runaway train."

"And you derailed it."

His laugh held a trace of bitterness. "Actually, it was Vicky who called the wedding off." Andrea lifted her brows in surprise. "A few weeks before the wedding, she confessed that she was having an affair with her boss."

"Oh, how awful!" She laid a comforting hand on his thigh and he quickly covered it with his own.

"The worst part was that the guy was both married *and* a friend of her father's. She pleaded with me to keep her secret. If the news got out, it would have created an unbelievable scandal, ruined her career, his career, etc., etc."

Andrea's admiration for him heightened. "So . . . you took the blame in order to save her reputation." She shook her head sadly. "You must have been devastated."

"Actually, once I got over the initial shock, my reaction was more a feeling of . . . well, relief. All of a sudden I realized that marrying Vicky was what other people wanted for me, what our families took for granted. It also made me recognize my love for her was that of a treasured friend." He moved closer to Andrea and traced her lips with his fingers. "I never felt this way about her. I've never felt this way about anyone."

When his lips closed on hers, Andrea eagerly returned his kiss and tingled with the desire that mounted within her once again. His hands were inside her shirt, cool against her skin. She pulled away long enough to shrug the material off and say in a throaty whisper, "You think taking your clothes off again will be a problem?"

He unsnapped his shirt. "No, but it could be habit-forming."

The high-pitched whine of a chainsaw split the early morning calm, waking Madison with a start. He propped himself on one elbow and blinked into a shaft of brilliant sunlight. The flawless blue sky made it difficult to believe there had ever been a storm.

Although it was barely seven o'clock, he had no doubt it was the people from the Forest Service busy clearing the fallen trees from the road. He knew they'd have a radio in the truck and could contact the authorities to let Marion know they were all right.

He glanced down at Andrea curled next to him, still sleeping peacefully. Careful not to wake her, he gently tucked the shirt around her. He quelled the urge to run his hand over her bare thighs, all the while relishing the images of their lovemaking the night before.

Quietly, he slipped into his clothes, tiptoed to the door and had his fingers on the handle when her sleepy voice stopped him.

"So, I'm to be seduced and abandoned?"

He turned to admire her disheveled appearance as she reclined on the mattress. The dark checkered shirt made a pleasing contrast to her white skin. She was perfect, he thought. Just perfect. He crossed the room and eased himself down next to her. "If my memory serves me correctly, I would have to say it was *I* who was seduced."

Andrea's desire for him was instantly rekindled as he drew her into his arms.

"Want to go for three?" he whispered, letting his hands come to rest on her hips.

"Mmmmmmm." She wrapped her arms behind his neck and brought his lips down to hers. Lost in the magical sensations that ricocheted through her, setting every cell in her body on fire, Andrea wished she could stop time, hold fast to the moment.

Her eyes flew open when she heard the shriek echo through the forest. "What was that?"

"A chain-saw. I'm afraid reinforcements from the Forest Service have arrived to clear the road and return us to civilization."

His remark burst the dreamy bubble that seemed to surround them, and jolted her back to reality. She pictured herself descending the stairs to a waiting audience of uniformed men, all staring at her with knowing eyes, gleaning from her face the vision of two naked bodies intertwined in love.

"Oh, my God, I've got to get dressed!" she cried, pushing Madison away and struggling to get to her feet.

"Relax," he said, chuckling, as he tried to restrain her. "No one even knows we're here."

"Oh, my legs!" she cried, collapsing back onto the mattress and rubbing her thighs.

"Here, let me do that," he said, massaging her gently. "I'm so sorry. I had a feeling you'd be suffering the ravages of yesterday's ride."

Andrea winced. "I don't think I can stand another two or three hours in the saddle."

Madison pursed his lips in thought. "Tell you what. Those guys are probably less than half a mile from here and I'm sure they'll have a radio. While you're getting dressed, I'll get a message to Marion to bring the truck and horse trailer. That way you won't have to ride at all."

Andrea hesitated. The thought of straddling a horse made her want to scream, but conversely, she had no desire to wait alone in the forest. "I'll go with you," she said, forcing herself to stand. "Do women still ride sidesaddle?"

He gave her a wide grin. "If Abigail doesn't object, neither do I."

Twenty minutes later, Andrea suppressed a groan as Madison helped her mount and drape her right leg around the pommel. She gave him a feeble smile. "Oh, thank you, Sir," she said in her best Southern twang. "I've always depended on the kindness of strangers."

He laughed as he adjusted the stirrup higher, then looked up at her expectantly. "Think you can handle this for a few minutes?" He swung onto his horse, his heart swelling with admiration. This woman had spunk.

As they rode, Andrea gritted her teeth against the relentless ache in her legs and congratulated herself. She'd certainly come a long way from the pampered socialite of a year ago.

After a few minutes, her discomfort subsided and she drew in deep breaths of the crisp, rain-washed air. Had the sky ever been this blue before? Had the sun ever seemed so bright? They rode in companionable silence, listening to the soft chirping of birds and exchanging several meaningful glances which left her feeling so happy, she thought she might burst.

At the sight of the Forest Service truck, she felt an unexpected twinge of doubt, and cast a quick glance at Madison. Alone with him in the tower, she'd felt safe, confident of her feelings, sure of his love, the outside world forgotten. But suddenly reality sunk in. What had she let herself in for? How could she have permitted herself to fall for the one man on earth who could drive a permanent wedge between her and Mo? She wondered if she could summon up the strength she needed to survive the problems that lay ahead.

"I think the rescue squad is here," Madison said as the red truck rounded the bend an hour later. They returned Marion and Christopher's frantic waves and heard the boy's exuberant shouts of joy as she screeched to a halt in front of them and rolled down the window.

"Madison McKee, you deserve forty lashes for giving us all such a scare!" Marion admonished, the expression of mock anger belying her brimming delight.

He threw her a good-natured grin as he opened the door. Christopher scrambled over her lap and Madison swung him to the ground.

"Am I glad to see you!" Andrea cried, dropping to one knee and gathering the boy in a tight squeeze.

After they embraced, Christopher drew back, his eyes wide. "I thought you were lost in the woods."

"We weren't lost, honey. The storm was too strong for us to get back, that's all."

"I had a pretty good idea you'd find your way to the old tower," Marion said, climbing down while giving Madison a sly look that caused Andrea's face to flush.

"Yep. Lucky we found a dry place," he said matter-of-factly, smoothly covering his discomfort as he began to untether the horses.

"Guess what, Andie?" Christopher announced excitedly, pulling her face to him. "I got to sit in the sheriff's car and listen to the radio when they were looking for you!"

"Well, this has turned out to be quite an adventure for you, what with the cattle branding and everything," she exclaimed, welcoming the change of subject.

"The kid's a natural cowboy," Marion called out over her shoulder as she helped load the pawing, snorting horses into the trailer.

"I'll drive," Madison said, sliding behind the wheel and beckoning Andrea to sit beside him. Marion climbed in last and took Christopher on her lap. While she was busy fiddling with the seatbelt, Madison gave Andrea's thigh a playful squeeze. She turned to him and met the wicked glow in his eyes. A tingle of joy raced through her, raising a host of goosebumps on her arms.

He drove slowly, dodging wide pools of water and deep crevices in the rutted dirt road.

"Thank you so much for taking care of Christopher," Andrea said, turning to Marion.

"Piffle!" she said, waving away the compliment. "It was fun getting to be a mom again." She gave the boy an affectionate hug.

Christopher leaned back against her ample bosom, looking contented, but after a moment his expression grew somber. "Mommy called last night. I told her you were lost and she was really scared," he said to Andrea.

"Oh dear. I was afraid of that."

"I did my best to put her mind at ease," Marion interjected. "By the way, her surgery is scheduled for . . ." She glanced at her watch. "Just about now."

Andrea tried to calm the gnawing dread that invaded her stomach. Once again, the disquieting knowledge that Mo's tumor might be malignant tempered her euphoric mood and increased her sense of guilt for feeling so happy, while her friend lay in a hospital bed miles away. It was an immense comfort when Madison's arm slid around her shoulders.

"Everything is going to be fine," he said, flashing her an encouraging smile.

Voicing her doubts would only serve to frighten Christopher, so she forced down the lump of fear that clogged her throat. "Your mom's going to be good as new," she said, taking his small hand in her own.

As they continued toward the ranch, Madison made no move to pull his arm away. Andrea's sideways glance at Marion to gauge the reaction to her brother's open display of affection was rewarded with a bold wink of approval.

She leaned her head back against the seat and let the tension flow from her body. If the news about Mo was indeed optimistic, and an agreeable settlement regarding Sundial House was reached, her own future, which had seemed murky only a week ago, now looked bright and hopeful.

It was mid-morning before they stepped out of the truck in front of the ranch house.

"May I use the phone?" Andrea asked anxiously as Madison and his sister unlatched the horse trailer.

"Go right ahead. Use the one in the living room," Marion said, waving her toward the door.

Her chest tight with apprehension, Andrea rushed inside and immediately called the hospital in Houston. When Mo's aunt told her the operation was completed and the tumor removed. It was not malignant, her knees crumpled with relief. She sat down hard in a chair, unable to curb the tears of joy that streamed down her cheeks.

"Is everything all right?" Madison asked, walking into the room as she cradled the phone.

She pushed to her feet. "Yes! The tumor was benign."

He folded her in his arms, his voice thick with emotion. "I'm glad as I can be, Andie."

Calling her by her nickname for the first time sent a thrill of delight through her and she reveled in the comfort of his embrace.

With reluctance, she disengaged herself from his arms when she heard Marion and Christopher enter the house.

"Guess what?" she exclaimed as they appeared in the doorway. "Your mommy's gonna be okay!"

The boy let out a joyous whoop and tried without success to execute several cartwheels.

Marion's face beamed with pleasure. "That's just wonderful! Andrea, could I interest you in a nice hot bubble bath before lunch?"

"That sounds like heaven ... but ... I don't know if there's time." She shot a hesitant glance at Madison.

"Take all the time you need," he said with an engaging smile and reached for the phone. "I'll call my office."

Madison's thoughts wandered as he slid the reference volume back into the bookshelf. What an extraordinary weekend it had been. Reliving the ecstasy in the fire tower, he could still envision Andrea's supple body, feel the softness of her in his arms, taste the sweetness of her. He returned to his desk humming, *Row, row, row your boat*— the final tune they'd all harmonized right before he'd dropped Andrea and Christopher off.

"I'm glad someone's happy around here," McKee, Sr. announced from the doorway."

Madison looked up, startled. "Dad! What are you doing here?"

His father closed the door and dropped into the upholstered leather chair facing him. "I've been trying to reach you all day."

"I got delayed in Sedona. There was a big storm last night in case you haven't heard."

"I heard. I heard. How's Marion?"

"Same as always."

McKee Sr. drummed the desk with his fingertips.

"I can see you've got something on your mind, Dad."

"Russ wants to know what the hold-up is. You've had this case for a week and nothing's happening."

"Hey! The other guys had it for a year."

"Yeah. And they got fired."

Madison wagged his finger at his father. "You're pushing, Dad. Give me some slack. I took this as a favor to you. Let me handle it my way."

"Okay, I'm sorry. But, I need to give Russ a progress report. Is the Callaway woman going to sign over the property or not?"

"Tell him there's been an unexpected delay. She's gone

into the hospital for surgery. When she gets out, I'll get on it."

He hated to admit to himself that he'd been too busy pursuing Andrea to give the case his full attention. He didn't have the foggiest idea how he would resolve it without bloodshed. He'd have to do that as soon as he got back from Tucson.

There was a light knock at the door and Blanche Kittering walked in. "Papers on the Stanton case," she said, waving some folders. "Scott just sent them over. Do you want to look at them now?"

Madison eyed his watch. "I should already be in Tucson. Is there anything that can't wait until I get back?"

She shrugged and placed the stack in front of him. "I guess not."

"I bet you miss me. Don't you, Blanche?" McKee, Sr. said with a wicked smile, reaching to pat her behind.

"Every day," she said, slapping his hand away. She directed a knowing look at Madison over her reading glasses before turning to leave.

McKee Sr. perked up, eyeing the folders with interest. "Anything I can help you with, Son?"

"Dad, you're retired, remember? Don't you have a date with your golf clubs or something?

"Played eighteen holes today already."

"I've got to get on the road," he said, rising from his seat and draping his arm around his father's shoulders as they moved to the door.

"You go on." He gave Madison a crafty grin. "I'm going to hang around a bit and give Blanche a hard time."

Chapter Nine

By Wednesday afternoon Andrea was still bathed in the hazy afterglow of her romantic encounter with Madison. Although his calls from Tucson were agonizingly brief, each one served to reinforce her growing love for him. She hummed a happy little song to herself as she headed for the main kitchen area. If all went well with his case, he'd be back by tomorrow afternoon and would call her the minute he got in. She could hardly wait.

In addition, Mo's rapid recovery lifted a great weight from her shoulders. She and Christopher were already caught up in plans for a welcome home party.

Andrea finished her conversation with the cook concerning the dinner menu and had just entered the foyer when the phone rang. As she reached for the receiver, she caught a glimpse of her dreamy expression in the antique mirror. Her skin had a radiant glow and she couldn't seem to get rid of the smile on her face.

"Hey, kiddo, you making me lots of money?"

"Mo! You sound great! You must be feeling better."

"Not a hundred percent, but at least my head isn't pounding like a kettle drum anymore. I paid the price though, I'm bald as a cue ball. How do you think I'll look in a blonde wig?"

"Ravishing. What's more important is you're well again. We can't wait to have you home."

"Ditto. Now, fill me in on what's happening there. Any interesting mail?"

"Hang on a second. It's back on your desk."

Andrea rushed to the office, picked up the extension and read the return addresses on the envelopes to Mo as she sifted through them.

"Whoa! Back up. The one from the city. Read that to me."

Andrea tore open the envelope. "It's an agenda for a meeting at the city council on Thursday."

"Damn! That's tomorrow. I was hoping the final arguments for the rezoning case would be postponed until I got back."

There was a long silence. "Mo?"

"I'm here. I'm thinking." Andrea didn't miss the note of consternation in her friend's voice. "Hmmmm. This is a toughie. Seems like I've done nothing but put you on the spot since you got here last week but ... I've got to ask you to do me one last favor, and it's a big one."

"Ask away."

She heard Mo sigh. "I need you to go there tomorrow and represent me, but I want to be sure you can handle it."

"Why, what would I have to do?"

"I already have my presentation prepared. It's in the folder in the bottom drawer. All you have to do is read it."

"Why wouldn't I be able to handle that?"

"Because . . . you'll probably be pitted against you-know-who, and from the little I do remember of what you said the other day, if what I think happened between you two when you were out there alone there in the woods, did happen . . . well . . ."

Andrea suppressed a twinge of uneasiness at the insinuation and cut in quickly, "Don't you worry your little head. It says here the meeting is scheduled for eleven A.M. and Madison won't even be back in town until tomorrow afternoon. Besides, maybe this won't turn out as badly as you think."

"Why? What did he tell you?"

Andrea hesitated. No matter how she tried to fool herself into thinking that it wasn't so, she'd managed to trap herself in the middle of this seemingly no-win battle. "He promised me he would try to resolve it to everyone's satisfaction."

"And you believe him?" Mo's voice rang with sarcasm.

Andrea's heart sank. At that moment she hated herself for loving Madison. "Whatever happens, you know I'm always on *your* side."

"Thanks a bunch, kiddo. I'm counting on that. Call me tomorrow after the meeting. Adios!"

"Wait! You haven't told me when you're coming back."

"The doctor thinks I'll be up to traveling by Saturday."

"That's super! I know one little boy who's going to be awfully happy to see you."

"It can't come too soon for me either."

Andrea had barely cradled the phone when it rang again.

"Andrea, please," said a woman's voice.

"Speaking."

"Oh, hi. This is Shirley Wilcox from tennis last week. Some of us gals are trying to get a doubles game for this evening if we can get a fourth. Are you interested?"

"What time?"

"Seven. Is that okay?"

She already had Debbie lined up to sit for Christopher and everything seemed to be running smoothly at the restaurant. "As far as I know it should be fine. But give me your number, Shirley, in case things get hectic around here and I can't make it." Andrea jotted down the number as Rose bustled in the door carrying a big box. "Whew! Those people sure know how to give you the runaround."

"What have you got there?" Andrea asked.

"The guest checks. They were supposed to be ready last week." She laid the box on the desk with a dramatic thump and collapsed into the chair, wiping beads of perspiration from her forehead.

"You look tired. Now I feel guilty for accepting a tennis invitation for this evening."

"Nonsense. You've worked like a slave these past two days. We have light reservations tonight and Lee will be here any minute to take care of the phones. I'm just going to sit here, do the books and catch up on back filing."

Andrea tapped her on the shoulder and picked up the money pouch. "Thanks, Rose. I'll make the bank deposit before I get Christopher from school."

Madison loosened his tie and undid the stiff collar of his shirt as he maneuvered the Range Rover through knots of rush hour traffic clogging the Tucson streets. If the freeway wasn't too crowded, he'd be back in Phoenix before dark.

He pushed an Elton John CD into the player and gave a deep sigh of satisfaction. All the parties in the case had been able to reach a workable compromise at the last minute, thus avoiding the court battle he'd geared up for. He'd wanted to call Andrea again to tell her he'd be getting in a day early, but decided to wait and surprise her. With luck, she'd have time to see him tonight. His blood surged at the thought of taking her in his arms again.

They'd only been apart a little over two days, but it felt

like forever. He was still overwhelmed by his feelings for her. He felt young and reckless, so utterly different from his usually controlled manner.

Getting back to Phoenix early would also mean he'd be able to make the Council Meeting in the morning himself, rather than send his associate to represent the firm.

Madison reached for the visor to block out the blinding rays of the late afternoon sun and his stomach coiled with elation when he thought again about the idea that had occurred to him last night. If Russell Stanton and Maureen Callaway would both agree to it, the problem of what to do with Sundial House would be solved. More than anything, he wanted to share his plan with Andrea, but decided it would not be prudent until he'd had a chance to convince Russell. He didn't even want to think about what would happen to the relationship between him and Andrea if he couldn't work things out.

It was ten to seven when Madison unlocked the private elevator and stepped into his penthouse apartment. The lingering odor of ammonia told him that the cleaning lady had been in earlier. He flung his suit jacket over the back of the bleached oak armchair, grabbed the cordless phone and crossed the expanse of white tile toward the balcony.

He tugged the vertical blinds and slid open the arcadia door with one hand while dialing Andrea's number with the other, as he stepped outside. While he waited for someone to answer, he leaned against the wrought iron railing and marveled at the spectacular view he had of the city, no matter what time of day, what time of year. Spread out before him, encircled by jagged, purple mountains, lay the wide valley glittering like the Crown Jewels in the soft twilight. He vowed the next time he stood here, Andrea would be enjoying the sight with him.

Finally the hostess answered. He felt encouraged when she told him Andrea was not at the restaurant. She must be at home with Christopher, he decided. Perhaps he could persuade her to get a sitter and spend the evening with him. He swiftly dialed Maureen's house. The line was busy. Impatient, he redialed. Busy again.

He moved into the kitchen and snapped open a beer, still trying the number. As he was about to press the redial button once again, the phone rang in his hand.

"Hello," he answered expectantly.

"Mack?" He was startled to hear Victoria's voice.

"Hey, stranger, I haven't heard from you in a month of Sundays."

"Where have you been?" She sounded cross. "I've been trying to reach you for hours. I need to talk."

"I have to make one quick call then I'll buzz you right back."

"No! I can't discuss this on the phone. I'm at The Grille Room. How soon can you be here?"

Madison felt somewhat perplexed at Victoria's tone. She'd always been demanding, but never this forceful. Damn, he wished he hadn't answered. Seeing her tonight was not in the cards, but the urgent note in her voice disturbed him.

"Mack, did you hear me?"

"I have plans for tonight."

"Are you my friend or not?"

"That's a dumb question."

Apparently sensing his irritation, her voice took on a note of pleading. "I'm sorry, Mack. I know it's short notice, but . . . I must talk to you tonight. Please?"

Madison sighed heavily. "What am I bailing you out of this time?"

"Not on the phone. Here."

He consulted his watch. He'd give her one hour and if all went well, he'd still be able to see Andrea.

"Okay. I'll just take a few minutes to shower and

change." He hung up and tried Andrea's number again. The busy signal droned in his ear.

Madison paused in the doorway, his gaze sweeping the dimly-lit room until he spotted Victoria. Clad in bright red, she was seated near the front window waving to him. He nodded in response and threaded his way through the tables, stopping briefly to acknowledge acquaintances on the way.

He smiled to himself as he drew closer. Because of her celebrity status, Victoria never appeared in public unless dressed to the 9's, her white-blonde hair perfectly coifed, her make-up carefully applied, no matter what ailed her. She was nervously smashing a cigarette into the ashtray as he slid into the chair opposite her.

He shook his head in disapproval. "Are you aware that the rest of the world has stopped smoking?"

Her eyes blazed with irritation. "I'm really not in the mood for a lecture."

He studied her more closely. The dark circles made her amber eyes appear almost cat-like. She looked pale. Something was very wrong.

"Nice to see you too, Vicky," he said quietly, folding his hands in front of him.

"Sorry, Mack." Her fingers trembled slightly as she lifted the Martini glass to her lips and took a long sip.

"How've you been?"

He smiled. "I'm fine, but I gather you're not. What's the crisis?"

Her eyes misted with tears. "I have a terrible, horrible decision to make and I don't know what to do."

"More horrible than canceling our wedding?"

"Oh, stop! You can't begin to know the guilt I've suffered for breaking up the families." She dabbed at her eyes with her napkin while giving him a sheepish smile. "And for letting you shoulder the blame all this time."

"Well, my shoulders are a lot bigger than yours."

She shook her head. "They threw away the mold when they made you."

"That's true," he said, feigning conceit.

She looked down when the waiter approached their table. "Another Martini, Ma'am?" he asked, removing her empty glass.

She nodded.

"Sir?"

"I'll have the same, and bring me a grilled chicken salad as well." He turned to Victoria. "Have you eaten?"

She shook her head.

"Make that two."

There was a moment of silence after the waiter left, then Madison reached across the table and took her hand. "Okay, let's have it."

"It's about Derek."

He rolled his eyes. "What a surprise." He released her hand and leaned back in his chair. "Let me guess. It took a smart girl like you four long years to realize he'll never leave his wife."

She thrust her chin forward defiantly. "Wrong!"

Madison drew back in surprise. "Oh?"

She fumbled for another cigarette and lit it. "Yes, and that's the problem. Can you imagine what my life's been like these past years? The holidays alone, canceled dates at the last minute, seeing him at parties and pretending we're just co-workers, sneaking around everywhere, the whole damn cloak and dagger existence! Oh, God, it's all been so . . . degrading."

"Whoa! You've lost me. He's finally leaving his wife and you're upset? Why? Is he dumping you for someone else?"

"No, Mack. He wants to marry me."

He threw up his hands in exasperation. "Vicky, quit talking in riddles."

She picked up her cigarette, inhaled and blew out a long stream of smoke. "I found out a few days ago that his wife is pregnant."

Madison gave a low whistle. "He told you he wanted to marry you, but now he's changed his mind."

"No, but now I'm not sure I want *him.*"

"Come on, Vicky, You didn't really believe he wasn't sleeping with his wife."

She blinked away fresh tears. "How could I have been so stupid? I was so positive this was the man I wanted. And to think what I did to you," she said, looking at him mournfully.

"It's all water under the bridge now."

"What should I do, Mack?"

Madison reached for her hand again. "Do you still love him?"

"Yes. But, I don't know if I like him anymore. It's not only because he lied to me, but what kind of a man would leave a pregnant wife?"

Madison gave her a level stare. "I think you just answered your own question."

She said nothing for several seconds, just stared back at him. Then she rose and moved behind his chair, draping her arms around his neck. "You're the greatest, you know that?"

He patted her gently on the arm. "You're not so bad yourself."

"Gotta go powder my nose," she said, sniffing. She took a step, then suddenly turned and kissed him full on the lips. "And to think what I gave up."

Andrea tossed the tennis racket into the back seat and eased behind the wheel, waving good-bye to Shirley as her car left the parking lot. She rolled down the window and filled her lungs with the soft night air, infused with the delicate scent of honeysuckle. It was a beautiful night. Everything was beautiful. Removing the visor, she absently fluffed her hair and took a deep, cleansing breath. She felt invigorated from the game and almost giddy with anticipation at the prospect of seeing Madison when he returned from Tucson tomorrow.

As she slid the key into the ignition, she looked toward the clubhouse dining room directly in front of her. The young couple seated at the table by the window, holding hands, caught her eye. The blonde woman, dressed in red, got up and moved around the table, draping her arms around the the man's neck. When she planted a kiss on his lips, Andrea smiled dreamily. How good love felt.

It was not until they drew apart and the man turned his face to the window that her heart faltered. She craned her head forward. No, it couldn't be. Madison wasn't even in Phoenix. "Oh, my God!" she whispered aloud. It *was* him!

The intoxicating halo of beauty that had surrounded her these past few days suddenly closed in, suffocating her, shattering around her like walls of glass.

She gripped the steering wheel as her mind frantically tried to expel the horror her eyes were witnessing. She wanted to flee, but sat frozen in shock, unable to move, unable to breathe.

Remembering his touch, his passion, their pledge of love for each other, she tried to make some sense of this living nightmare. She'd trusted him. How could he have been so cruel as to toy with her emotions? And why? Why had he lied? How could he have led her to believe that she was the only one? What a fool she'd been. Hadn't she learned anything from her experience with Bernard, his treachery, his manipulation?

The despair in her heart and the churning in her stomach became one monstrous, gouging pain inside her. It was as though there'd been yet another death in her life.

She'd been unaware of anyone nearby until she felt the door from the adjacent car bump into hers. The tumultuous feelings that had been building inside her came together in an explosion of rage. "Are you out of your mind?" she shrieked to the bewildered man standing next to her in the semi-darkness. "Have you no respect for other people's property?"

"I . . . I'm sorry," he stammered. "I was just trying to get into my car." He smoothed his hand along the paint on her door. "It was barely a tap. There's no harm done."

With the realization that she was unfairly transferring her anger onto this innocent stranger, she opted for a hasty retreat. Shoving the car into reverse, she squealed backward and peeled out of the parking lot, tormenting herself with thoughts of how she'd encouraged Madison, actually seduced him. She'd never done anything so wanton, so brash before in her life. Was it because they'd been at the mercy of the elements that her resistance had weakened, or was it the intimate seclusion, the firelight, the fact that she was so cold and frightened, that she'd needed his closeness to warm her?

"None of the above, you fool," she sobbed. *Admit it, Andrea. You let your guard down because you love this man, pure and simple.*

She drove aimlessly, oblivious to time and space until, miraculously, she ended up at Mo's house with no memory of how she got there. Dropping her forehead onto the steering wheel, she sat motionless for a few minutes, until the screen door squeaked open. She looked up to see Debbie silhouetted in the doorway.

"Are you all right?" the girl asked.

Just great, Andrea thought. "I'm fine. Sorry I'm late," she said, sliding out of the car.

Debbie held the door open for her as she trudged up the stairs and went inside.

"How'd everything go?" Andrea asked wearily.

"Just dandy. Christopher was in bed by eight." The girl pulled on her shoes, gathered her books from the couch and walked toward the door. "By the way, Mo called to remind you about the meeting tomorrow."

"Oh, I forgot the file," she mumbled.

"Rose dropped it off. I left it on the coffee table," she said over her shoulder as she went out the door.

Andrea tiptoed into Christopher's room and gently tucked the sheet around him. She watched him sleeping peacefully, then left the room, envying his innocence, wishing she were a small child again with only small problems.

She roamed listlessly through the house, tortured by her thoughts, wondering whether there was a plausible explanation for what she'd seen at the clubhouse. What was she doing, making excuses for him?

Stepping out onto the front porch, memories of that first evening with Madison invaded her mind. Absently, she stroked the railing they'd leaned against as they talked. Her throat clogged as she remembered his tender kiss.

She looked up at the sky. There'd been a full moon that night, beaming its blessing down on them. All that remained of that moon now was a thin sliver of light as though it was cowering, retreating from its part in the conspiracy against her, leaving behind a heavy cloak of melancholy.

The sudden jangle of the phone shattered the silence. Before she could reach it, she heard the answering machine click on and froze in her tracks at the sound of Madison's voice.

"Hi, it's me. I finished up in Tucson earlier than expected and I've been trying to reach you, hoping I could see you tonight. I can't wait to show you how much I've missed you. Call me the minute you get in."

She stood still, as though in a stupor. Then anger began to well inside her as she dropped into a chair and banged her fist on the machine. To her horror, she reactivated the message and the deceitful words came pouring out again.

"Stop it! Stop it!" she hissed through clenched teeth, pulling at her hair to arrest the scream that rose in her throat.

"Damn you, damn you, you liar." The words triggered an avalanche of tears and, for what seemed like hours, she sat weeping, surrendering completely to her grief.

After the racking sobs subsided, she sat unmoving in the chair, staring into the darkness until a blessed numbness began to flow through her, bequeathing a curious sense of strength. She'd lived through unhappiness before, she would survive. Squaring her shoulders, she rose from the chair and headed for bed, knowing that she'd already begun the arduous process of resurrecting the protective fortress around her heart.

Chapter Ten

Christopher's voice gradually seeped into Andrea's mind, still mired in sleep. She wanted to open her eyes, but couldn't. Her lids felt as if they were weighted down with anchors, her limbs felt weak.

"Andie, wake up!"

Feeling as though she were climbing from the depths of a deep, dark well, she willed her way to the surface of consciousness and slowly lifted her lashes, laboring to focus on the little boy's puzzled face.

"Why are you sleeping in the chair?"

Disoriented, she squinted into a shaft of bright morning sunlight and glanced around the living room. "I must have dozed off," she mumbled and started to rise, then let out a cry of dismay as she watched the folder slide from her lap. The enclosed papers scattered across the hardwood floor with a swish. "Oh, no!"

"It's okay," Christopher said, quickly dropping to his knees. "I'll help you."

"No, that's all right." She glanced at the mantel clock

and saw that it was after seven. She'd slept for two hours. "You start getting ready for school."

She gave a heavy sigh when he'd left the room and began to gather the papers, striving to hold onto the soothing numbness the brief nap had granted her. But it was to no avail. Even though she struggled against it, the vision of Madison kissing the attractive blonde penetrated her thoughts, generating a feeling of such profound loss that she suffered actual physical pain.

She was positive last night had been the longest on record. After a few hours of tossing and turning, she'd abandoned any hope of sleep and returned to the living room to study the file. Focusing her efforts on Mo's problem had helped to busy her mind and stem the pain that coiled around her heart like a poisonous snake.

After collecting the documents, Andrea rose stiffly to her feet, knowing it would take every ounce of her determination to concentrate on the task ahead. She tried to push aside the disquieting notion that, not only was she being called upon to make a public speech for the first time in her life, but that she would be confronting Madison McKee.

She hurried into the kitchen and set out cereal and fruit for Christopher, then dashed into the bathroom. There was barely enough time to shower before she'd have to drive him to school.

Her grief and anxiety, coupled with the spell of comatose-like sleep, left her feeling lethargic and fuzzy-headed, as though she'd taken a sedative. She turned the cold water tap and deliberately endured the chilling spray until she felt somewhat revived.

Christopher looked up from his breakfast and smiled at her when she came into the kitchen. "Madison called. I told him you were in the shower," he said, cramming the last bite of banana into his mouth.

Andrea caught her breath and stood staring at him, her

heart banging hard against her rib cage. "What did he say?"

"He said he'll see you later."

"A lot sooner than he thinks," she muttered under her breath, remembering how she'd naively shrugged off Mo's warning that she might be pitted against him. What cruel irony!

When she returned after dropping Christopher at school, Andrea checked in with Rose, then resolutely turned down the volume on the answering machine in case Madison called again. She'd check the messages later. In her overwrought state of mind, hearing his voice would be more than she could bear; besides she needed a clear head to sort out Mo's material.

She brewed a pot of strong coffee before spreading out the jumble of papers on the kitchen table. Her heart sank. If there hadn't been so little time, she would have been amused at Mo's description of her 'prepared speech' which was in actuality a series of *Post-it notes* attached to various zoning documents criss-crossed with arrows. How was she ever going to make sense of this mess?

For a while she just sat feeling helpless, staring out the window, listening to the birds twitter. She'd have to get it together somehow. Mo was depending on her. Summoning inner strength, she began to painstakingly piece the notes together.

She held her breath when the phone rang, her delicate resolve threatening to crumble. She knew it was Madison and ached to answer the call, to believe that he still loved her. Instead, she gritted her teeth against the intrusive sound and wrenched her thoughts back to the matter at hand, steeling her nerves for the unavoidable confrontation.

* * *

Madison waited another twenty minutes before calling Mo's house again. He was puzzled that Andrea hadn't returned his calls. Obviously, she hadn't checked for messages and still thought he was in Tucson.

He heard Mo's lilting voice on the recording again. "You know who I am, so tell me who you are and I'll call you back." He chuckled to himself. Too bad he hadn't met this lady under different circumstances. She was a real crack-up. "Andie, it's Madison again. I hope Christopher gave you my message. I'll try you later at the restaurant."

He hung up, disappointed. He must have just missed her. Most likely she was en route to Christopher's school.

He shifted his thoughts to the development project. The anticipation of his idea's success made his heart rate climb. He grabbed up his car keys and headed down to the garage. It was imperative that he meet with the architect this morning to determine the feasibility of incorporating his inspired concept into the design before approaching Russell Stanton. If it could be done without compromising the plan, then he felt confident he'd be able to convince him. He wished there was time to do everything before the eleven o'clock meeting, but, since there wasn't, he would aim for a postponement of the final re-zoning decision.

Her stomach twisting into a quivering, squeamish knot, Andrea parked the car near the City Council Chambers and got out. She wished now she'd eaten something with the coffee, but the thought of food had nauseated her.

After a few deep breaths of air, thick with the odor of sun-baked asphalt, she walked with slow, deliberate steps toward the building.

She'd taken great pains to look her best, choosing a long-sleeved blouse of delicate pink silk to wear under her tailored cream suit. Not a good choice, she berated herself, convinced she'd burn up and blow away in the wind if she didn't get to a cool place soon.

Spotting Madison's Range Rover sent an electrifying charge through her, refueling her anger, re-energizing her flagging spirits, dispelling any doubt that she would accomplish what she'd set out to do.

It was a relief to step inside the air-conditioned building. The dimly-lit, circular room was laid out like an amphitheater. She slipped into the back row of seats, hoping to remain anonymous until it was time for her presentation. Any confrontation with Madison beforehand would be very detrimental to her fragile state of mind.

She surveyed the crowded room, searching for him as one would a dreaded opponent in battle and saw him in the front row, conferring with another man, their heads bent over a pile of papers. Unwittingly, she stared at his wavy hair, shining like a beacon under the overhead lights. She forced herself to look away, relieved that she couldn't see his face. Closing her eyes, she let her body go limp and took long, measured breaths to calm the anxiety that threatened to undermine her resolve.

When she heard the case number called, she sat up with a start and her heart thumped wildly as Madison approached one of the podiums that faced the council members.

She listened carefully as he gave a brief summary of the conflicting issues, then suppressed a gasp of surprise when she heard him remark, "In all fairness to Ms. Callaway, who is at present in the hospital and therefore unable to defend her point of view, I would like to request a fifteen-day postponement on this issue."

Andrea jumped to her feet. "I'm representing Ms. Callaway!" she cried, surprised by her bold tone.

Madison whirled in shock and stared at her wordlessly, feeling as though all the air had been punched from his lungs. He watched as she confidently strode to the second podium, astounded that she hadn't even looked at him, that she was there at all. She'd no sooner been recognized by the Council, than she launched into a merciless, scathing attack on the proposed development.

He retreated to his seat, puzzled and hurt, especially that her harsh criticism seemed to include him. What had come over her? He tried to catch her eye, but she resolutely turned her face away from him as her final words rang in his ears.

"Don't believe it when they say it's all in the name of progress. Let's call it by its real name, ladies and gentlemen—greed. Thank you for your time." At that, she swiveled and returned to her seat.

Madison could barely steady his voice as he rose and reiterated his request for postponement, citing possible new factors that could alter the outcome of the case. After conferring for a few minutes, the Council granted his request, then called the next item.

He hastily gathered up his material and, from the corner of his eye, watched her march toward the door. He clenched his jaw. She wasn't getting away until he found out what was going on. He loped up the aisle and followed her out, catching up with her a few feet from the curb.

"Andrea, wait!" Irritation heated his face as she ignored him and kept walking. He quickened his gait and grabbed her elbow, swinging her around to face him.

"What the hell's gotten into you?" The animosity in her eyes made him recoil in astonishment.

She jerked her arm away. "I have nothing to say to you."

He caught her again. "Just a minute. Don't you think I deserve some kind of explanation for this irrational behavior? When I called you from Tucson yesterday you said you loved me. And now you don't want to *talk* to me?"

"If you were there at all," she said with stinging sarcasm.

He drew back, unable to hide his shock. "What's that supposed to mean?"

She plucked his hand away and pulled herself up to her full height, impaling him with the venom in her blue eyes. "I refuse to play this game with you. I put up with a deceitful, manipulative man for eight years. I'm not going to do it again."

"What game? Do you want to give me a small clue as to what you're getting at?"

"Oh, please!" she said, rolling her eyes. "You may as well drop the innocent act. I'm not the naive fool you were talking to yesterday."

He raked his hand roughly through his hair. "The least you can do is tell me what I'm being accused of so I can attempt to clear myself."

"Okay." She inclined her head, fixing him with a cynical smile. "You could start with the charade about being in Tucson."

Madison's confusion heightened. "I *was* in Tucson."

"Oh, my mistake," she said with exaggerated politeness. "It must have been your ornery twin brother I saw snuggling with that woman at the tennis club last night."

Madison stared at her, speechless, as the realization sunk in, then threw back his head, laughing. "So, that's what this is all about."

His patronizing attitude infuriated her even more. "I'm sure for you, kissing women in public is no big deal."

"*I* wasn't kissing her. She was kissing *me.*"

"Oh, well then, that makes it entirely acceptable," she said, throwing up her hands.

Madison folded his arms over his chest. "For your information, Miss Jump-to-Conclusions, that was Vicky."

Andrea was thrown off guard by his unexpected announcement. "Is that supposed to make me feel better? Somehow in your detailed biography you apparently forgot to mention how terribly close the two of you still are."

He shook his head, exasperated, but now better able to justify her reaction. "I told you you were the only person in my life now and I meant it. Come on," he said, taking her arm, gently this time. "Let's go sit in the shade while I explain it all to you." He caught her skeptical look. "If you need corroboration, I'll be glad to introduce you to Vicky."

She read the sincerity in his eyes and felt her anger diminish. "No, that won't be necessary."

"Good." He led her to a small wooden bench nestled beneath a tree with bright yellow blossoms.

As she sat listening to his explanation, she was overcome with embarrassment and cringed, recalling her unfair attack directed at him at the Council meeting.

She could hardly meet his eyes. "I guess I did jump to conclusions when I had no right . . ."

He put his fingertip under her chin, forcing her to look at him. "I understand why you did. But please do me the favor of not putting me in the same category as your lousy ex-husband."

She fidgeted with the folder on her lap, then flashed him a sheepish smile. "This is all backwards, you know. I never dreamed I'd end up owing you an apology today. Madison, I'm so sorry."

A wide grin lit his face. "Apology accepted. By the way, I have to take my hat off to you for such an accomplished presentation. You were magnificent," he said, gazing at her with undisguised admiration. "I just wish the brunt of it hadn't been directed against me."

"Why didn't you tell me you were trying to get the decision postponed?"

He raised a quizzical brow. "And when would I have done that?"

She thought of his calls she hadn't returned and felt duly chastened. "Good point."

He covered her hands with his. "Look, I came up with an idea last night that might save everybody's bacon. I can't divulge any details yet, because I'm not certain Russell

Stanton will go along with it. But I can tell you this much—if it works out the way I have it planned, the situation could turn out better than Maureen hoped.''

Andrea felt worse than ever that she'd doubted him. ''I feel dreadful for treating you so badly,'' she said with visible invitation in her eyes. ''How can I ever make it up to you?''

''I can think of a few ways.'' He gently removed a blossom that had fallen into her hair, then drew her close to him. ''Do you still object to public displays of affection?'' he whispered in her ear.

Flooded with happiness and relief she sighed, lifting her lips to his. ''Not anymore.''

Andrea sat in the waiting area of the airport, keeping one eye on Christopher, who had his face pressed to the glass watching for his mother's plane, while also observing the mélange of travelers and those clinging onto them. She smiled contentedly to herself as she watched couples locked in bittersweet embraces. As wonderful as love was, she knew now it was not always sweetness and light. But even with all the ups and downs she would opt for love anyday.

Making up with Madison made everything between them even more wonderful, more fulfilling. She thought back to the blissful hours they'd managed to capture together these past three days, especially that first night at his apartment after they'd quarreled. He'd carefully set the stage for an unforgettable evening, beginning with champagne and lobster on his candlelit balcony. Later on, the rapture of their impassioned lovemaking crowned the night.

''It's here! It's here!'' Christopher shouted, jumping up and down.

Andrea eagerly joined him at the window and squeezed his shoulders. ''Let's go stand by the doorway so we can see your mommy the minute she comes out.''

As she watched him skip ahead of her, she was reminded of the leisurely hours they'd spent earlier today at the park with Madison where the two had played and wrestled as though they were father and son.

She craned her head as the throng of passengers filed by, wondering what innovative solution Mo had dreamed up to camouflage her hairless condition, fully expecting her to make a spectacular entrance. She wasn't disappointed. Apart from her starkly pale complexion, there was Mo, wearing a silk purple turban with a matching feather attached to the winking rhinestone brooch in the center.

"What rich Maharajah willed you that?" Andrea asked with a laugh after the three had finished their marathon hugging.

She drew back and flamboyantly threw out her arms. "As long as I have to wear something, I'm entitled to make a statement." She raised a brow in mock seriousness. "You don't think it's too much, do you?"

"Heavens, no. I think you should have one in every color."

Mo knelt eye to eye with Christopher. "And what do you think, my little man?"

"You look like the genie from the bottle," he said, his face flushed with happiness.

Mo's outlandish appearance drew stares as they trekked through the crowded terminal out to the parking lot. During the short drive to the house, Christopher chattered nonstop about all the things he'd done while his mother had been away.

"It sure is good to be home," Mo remarked as they climbed the porch steps and swung open the front door. Christopher and Andrea exchanged a conspiratorial grin.

Mo's hands flew to her mouth when she saw the WELCOME HOME sign suspended from the living room ceiling, along with colorful streamers and balloons. "You guys are too much!"

"We have cake and ice cream!" Christopher squealed, pulling her to the dining room table.

Her eyes misted. "Thank you. You two are the greatest in the whole wide world, you know that?" She gave them each a noisy kiss, then dropped into a chair.

"Are you okay?" Andrea asked anxiously.

"Just a little tired. Cake and ice cream will perk me right up."

Andrea thought Mo looked relatively well after what she'd been through, in addition to the long airline flight.

"How is that terrific crew of mine doing?" Mo asked, gesturing toward Sundial House.

"Just great. They send their love."

"Maybe I ought to drop in to say hello."

"Be serious. Tomorrow's plenty soon enough."

Andrea had just dished up the dessert when the doorbell rang. "You two eat." She moved to open the door. "Oh, my goodness!" she said, finding herself confronted by a delivery boy holding a sumptuous basket of fruit. She thanked him and carried it to the table. "Will you look at this!"

"Is it from the gang?" Mo asked, expectantly.

"I don't know." She extended the small envelope to her.

A skeptical frown crossed Mo's face as she read the card. "Surprise, surprise. It's from Madison McKee." She gave a haughty sniff and set it aside.

Andrea sensed her displeasure, but said nothing until Christopher had gone to his room to watch television.

"Are you up to talking about Madison now?" she asked meeting Mo's gaze directly.

"I'm tired, but I wasn't about to hit the sack until you fill in all the blanks about your torrid night in the tree house."

"Fire tower."

"Whatever."

Under Mo's intense scrutiny, Andrea felt the blush heat her face as she recounted what happened.

"Is this a wild fling or is there something more serious going on here?"

"It's not a fling, but beyond that, I don't know. I have to take it one day at a time."

"I hate to rain on your parade, but where does this leave me with Sundial House?"

"Madison told me he's working on an idea. I don't know any details, but he said this could turn out better than you hoped."

"He must be a magician as well as a lawyer, because there's no way he could do me any favors when he's working for the other side." When Andrea said nothing, Mo reached across the table and laid a hand over hers. "You really love this guy, don't you?"

"I would have never dreamed it possible, and I certainly didn't plan it, but . . . yes, I do."

Mo blew out a long breath. "Oh, boy. You love him, Christopher's nuts about him, and I'm stuck right in the middle. Whatever I do will be wrong."

"It doesn't have to be. Give Madison the benefit of the doubt, Mo. If he does come up with a good plan, will you listen?"

Mo rose from her chair, yawning. "I'll sleep on it."

Chapter Eleven

Monday morning, Andrea marveled at how quickly Mo had recovered and settled back into her element. She watched with amusement and a deep sense of satisfaction as her friend waltzed around the restaurant, barking orders, taking charge of everything as though she'd never left. The only visible difference in her appearance was the auburn page boy wig with bangs that they'd shopped for yesterday.

As she followed Mo up the staircase to help rearrange seating for a private luncheon, she thought about how wonderful Sunday had been except for the fact that she hadn't heard from Madison. He'd most likely bowed out of the picture to allow Mo to get resettled and give them time to catch up on everything. Andrea wondered when he'd contact her with the details for ending the stalemate.

During dinner the night before, while Christopher gave his mother a glowing endorsement of Madison, Andrea had watched Mo's face and happily observed signs that she might be softening her rigid stance on Sundial House.

Mo had worn a thoughtful smile and listened without comment, which gave Andrea new hope that she might grant Madison and his proposal a fair hearing. She'd been dying to bring up the subject again, but had instead kept quiet. She needed to give Mo the chance to sort things through without undue influence from her.

"Look at all these incredible antique pictures!" Andrea exclaimed, opening the exquisite armoire that graced the top floor of the restaurant. "Why hide them away in here? Let's dust them off and hang them up for everyone to enjoy."

Mo made a face. "I don't have time for that. I've got a zillion things to catch up on first. We'll work on it next week." Her eyes widened with sudden alarm. "Oh, no, I just remembered! You won't be here next week." She hastily set the armload of fresh flowers on a table and hurried to Andrea's side. "Do you really have to go back on Friday?"

"You know I do. I've only got the weekend to get myself together before work on Monday. As it is, I'll have to hunt for a new apartment later."

Mo threw her a sideways glance. "What about Madison? Where does he fit into this picture?"

"I honestly don't know." That vexing question had haunted her whenever she'd let it, and now it spawned another pang of anxiety. Although Madison's love seemed genuine, he hadn't indicated where their relationship was going from here. He hadn't addressed any tangible commitment. Was he avoiding the subject? But more important, was she avoiding it?

"Hey, Mo!" Rose called from the bottom of the stairs. "Lydia Cramer's on the phone in your office."

"Thanks, Rose. Tell her to hang on." She turned to Andrea with a secretive gleam in her eye. "That's my spy who works down at the Municipal Building."

"Your spy?"

"Yeah. She keeps her eyes peeled for anything that's happening with this crazy zoning battle. I'll be back," she said, clattering down the polished wooden stairs.

Andrea absently placed a pat of butter on each bread plate as, alone with her thoughts, she mulled over her decision to leave on Friday. It made her heart ache to think of leaving Mo so soon after the surgery. And there was Christopher . . . But she knew it was more than that.

Last Thursday night at Madison's apartment while she lay in the dreamy haze that followed their lovemaking, he'd asked her why she had to go back to New York.

"Because I live there," she'd responded evasively, laughing off the implication of his question, while half hoping he'd ask her to stay and assure her that this all-consuming love was the beginning of something more permanent.

Yet his silence, his pensiveness, weighed heavily on her. But then, how could she fault him? One week of passion wasn't enough time for either of them to be sure it would last. No, they both needed more time. Perhaps putting some distance between them would let her evaluate the situation more objectively.

She sighed as she finished preparing the tables. "Why is love so complicated?" she questioned aloud, then, realizing Mo had not returned after the phone call, went down to the office to find her.

"What happened? I thought you were coming back." Her steps faltered when she noticed Mo sitting slumped at the desk, her hands pressed to her temples. Her pulse beat faster in her throat. "You're not having headaches again, are you?"

Mo shook her head and turned around, her face a ghostly white. "You'll never guess what I just heard."

Andrea felt a chill of foreboding as she eased herself slowly onto the couch. "What?"

"And to think I was actually willing to give him the benefit of the doubt! I tell you that guy is as slippery as

oysters on a china plate. Not only has he got you bamboo-
zled, the creep pretty near had me fooled too."

Andrea knew she was talking about Madison and sat,
stunned, waiting for the guillotine to drop.

"His clever ploy was working. Oh, yes. He charms you
into the sack, befriends Christopher ..." She clenched
her jaw, her face reddening with anger. "And all the while
he's busy digging my grave behind the scenes."

"Please don't do this to me. Just tell me what happened."

"Lydia Cramer said a request for condemnation of Sundial House just came across her desk. And, no, I don't
want to keep you in suspense, Andie, it's signed by Madison
McKee."

Madison finished signing the stack of letters that his
secretary had placed on his desk and leaned back to relax
his shoulders, enjoying the positive feelings that flowed
through him. With the exception of the few hours he'd
spent with Andrea and Christopher Saturday afternoon,
he'd worked practically nonstop over the weekend with
David Banks, Russell's architect. They'd pored over the
plans for the development until he thought his eyes would
give out. At first David had insisted the unorthodox idea
would compromise the design, but he'd finally come
around.

Madison smiled and ran his hand over the finished draw-
ings. David was worth every penny he'd paid him. He
glanced at his watch and braced himself for the challenge.
All he had to do now was sell the concept to Russell Stanton.

"Do you want me to set up the easel in the conference
room?" Blanche asked from the doorway.

"No, over there by the couch will be fine. There's only
going to be Russell, Dad and myself."

"Trish is busy with a deposition. Shall I get someone else to take the minutes?"

"Thanks, I don't think it'll be necessary."

When Blanche returned with the easel, Madison arranged the renderings in order. "Buzz me when Russell gets here," he called to her retreating figure.

After the four year vacuum in the relationship, he'd been nervous when he'd first placed the call to Russell Stanton, inviting him to come and hear his plan. But he'd been puzzled and pleasantly surprised by his receptive manner.

"Sure thing," Russell had said. "I'm meeting Victoria for lunch afterwards. Why don't both you and your dad join us?"

Even though everyone knew that he and Vicky had remained friends, Madison was still taken aback at Russell's suggestion. The unexpectedly cordial attitude would certainly make things easier. The prospect of dismantling the wall of animosity that separated the two families looked promising.

Blanche buzzed him on the intercom. "He's on his way."

Showtime! Madison straightened his tie and moved to the door, pulling himself erect to meet Russell Stanton's tall, sinewy presence. The two eyed each other warily for a brief second, then Madison initiated a firm handshake. "It's good to see you again, Russ."

"You did a smart thing to take this on," he said, fixing his steely-gray eyes on him. "It will go a long way toward setting things right."

"I sure hope so." He gestured for him to sit in the leather chair facing the easel. "Dad is on his way. Would you like coffee in the meantime?"

Russell settled himself comfortably. "Why not."

Madison leaned out the door and asked Blanche to bring it. At the same instant he saw his father step from the elevator and hurry toward him.

"Is everything copacetic?" McKee, Sr. muttered anxiously to his son.

Madison placed a hand on one shoulder and gave his father a reassuring smile. "No bullets have been fired yet."

McKee Sr. squared his shoulders as he sauntered into the office where he greeted Russell with an amiable embrace. "Almost feels like old times seeing you here," he said, seating himself next to him.

Russell's gaze swept the room. "Looks the same except for that garish new painting," he said with a tone of mischief.

Madison accepted the barb good-naturedly and held the door wide while Blanche brought in the coffee.

"Seeing you two boys together again is sure a sight for sore eyes," she said with an affectionate smile, setting the tray on the low table.

"And it's going to stay that way. Right, Son?" McKee Sr. gave Madison a sagacious stare.

Answering him with a slight nod, Madison winked his thanks to Blanche as she left the room, then stepped to the easel to begin his presentation.

"You've been at an impasse for over a year on this project, with both sides shrinking further and further from an agreement. That's no revelation to you, Russ, but the way things stand now, every day this is held up is costing you a bundle, which I know is not making your backers any too happy. And we don't have to go into the legal costs you've already racked up along the way. Agreed?"

"Go on."

He set the first rendering on the easel. "As you'll soon see, I've worked out what I feel will be an equitable solution which would bring all parties to the table. With a slight modification on the original design, my approach is not only feasible, but the numbers add up nicely to make it an all around good, solid deal."

Russell crossed one leg over the other, looking expectant. "I'm still listening."

"For the last forty-eight hours, David Banks and I have burned the midnight oil to come up with this." He flipped the page on the poster board revealing a full color illustration.

Russell's eyes narrowed. "What the hell is this? It's that damned house I'm trying to get rid of."

"Ah hah!" Madison brandished his finger with a flourish. "But, that's the beauty of this whole thing. You don't have to. Sundial House would be incorporated into the project!"

Russell stood up, looking doubtful, and moved to study the sketch more closely. "Keep talking."

Feeling encouraged that he hadn't rejected it out-of-hand, Madison continued quickly, "As you can see, it's a very aesthetic blend of old and new which I think puts a rather creative spin on the project. That's a big plus in the anti-development climate we have right now."

"Wait a minute! Where does the Callaway woman fit into this?"

"Simple. The idea is to persuade her to drop the rezoning fight and sign over the property for a small percentage of the development."

"I'd have to make that woman a partner?" he asked incredulously.

Madison put up a hand. "Hear me out on this. First of all, you get to side-step the buy-out costs. Secondly, you've got a built-in anchor that's already a proven money-maker. Sundial House has been number one on the business luncheon circuit three years in a row, besides being a popular landmark that pulls a hefty percentage of the tourist trade."

"But . . ."

"Keeping in mind the considerable amount of vacant office space available until the market turns around, you would be providing an automatic draw to potential ten-ants—an in-house perk, so to speak.''

Madison could tell by the calculating gleam Russell had in his eyes that he was totaling up the advantages. "Hmmmm, I don't know. It's pretty damned revolutionary. What do you think?" he asked, turning to McKee, Sr.

Madison looked at his father who'd been silent all this time and was surprised to see a guarded expression on his face. *Say something, Dad,* he urged silently. *Come on, back me up.*

"Well ..." he began cautiously, "there's something I oughta clue you two in on and ..."

They all turned as the door swung open and Blanche leaned in. "Madison, David Banks is on three."

He threw her an irritated glance. "I'm in the middle of something. Tell him I'll call him back."

She fixed him with a meaningful glare. "You'd better talk to him now."

The urgency in her manner filled Madison with sudden concern. He excused himself and crossed to the desk to answer the call.

"David. What is it?" He pressed the phone to his ear and listened with disbelief. "When? I never authorized that. I was in Tucson!" He listened intently for another minute while locking eyes with his father. "Thanks, I'll get back to you." He slammed down the phone and strode over to his father, fighting to control the anger that was building inside him. "I don't suppose you know how a certain condemnation request got down to the City, do you, Dad?"

"I was just about to tell you. You were busy, you were going out of town . . . I was just trying to help things along."

"Damn it, Dad ..." He clenched his fists and forced himself to restrain the tirade that threatened to pour out.

"Hold it a minute," Russ cut in. "Are we talking about Sundial House?"

"Yes, we are," Madison growled, still glaring at his father.

"Whoa, now. Let's not be too hard on your old dad here," he said with a crafty look. "Our troubles are over. We don't have to go through all this rigamarole now." He pointed to the easel. "Just let the City do its stuff and condemn the place and we're home free." He gave a self-satisfied grin. "Little Missy Callaway will be history."

"Oh sure. That would be rich!" Madison said caustically. "The press will have a field day. I can just see it now," he said, spreading an imaginary headline in front of him. "LOCAL GOLIATH UPROOTS HELPLESS MOTHER AND YOUNG SON." He laughed bitterly. "And that's not the half of it. You'll have the Historical Society on your back, the women's organizations in an uproar, the Inner-City Small Business Association in a rage, not to mention the heat you'll get from the neighborhood groups that will rally around her."

Russell's face grew scarlet. He turned to McKee Sr., who looked like he wanted to dissolve into the chair. "I *never* should have listened to you!" he shouted. "Your so-called brilliant son has gone soft, if you ask me." He now faced Madison, his eyes flashing fire. "What you did to me and my daughter, canceling the wedding, has stuck in my craw for four long years. You made a fool of me once, and I sure as hell am not going to let you do it again by screwing up this deal for me. You know something, Madison? I'm *glad* you're not my son-in-law."

Suddenly, all the color drained from Russell's face as he looked toward the open doorway. "Victoria! When did you get here?"

When she replied, it was as though she had ice in her eyes and voice. "If you weren't fighting like boys in a schoolyard, you would have heard me come in."

An uncomfortable silence fell over the room as she closed the door quietly behind her and strode in with a resolute expression on her face. "I should have done this a long time ago, but I guess now is as good a time as any."

Madison put out his hand. "Vicky, don't."

She shrugged off his plea. "No. The charade stops here."

"Victoria, stay out of this," Russell ordered.

"Father, sit down." The fierce note in her voice silenced him and he dropped into the chair.

"To set the record straight, Madison didn't break off the wedding. I did."

"What?" Russell's mouth gaped open.

Madison started to intervene, but Victoria shook her head violently. "It's time."

As the truth poured from her lips, Madison couldn't help but feel a wicked sense of satisfaction seeing Russell chastened by his daughter's revelation, then drop his head into his hands. After a few agonizing moments he raised his face to hers.

"Oh, Victoria," he groaned. She said nothing while desolation clouded his eyes. "Am I such an unsympathetic bastard that you couldn't level with me? Don't you know that my only child's happiness has always meant more to me than anything else in the world?"

She moved to his side and perched on the armrest of his chair. Tears swam in her eyes as she draped an arm around his shoulder. "It's not you, Dad. I was too ashamed to tell you. Worse still, I've been a sniveling coward up until now. So you see," she sighed, "I think you and I both owe Madison a good deal more than a simple apology."

Father and daughter exchanged a long, meaningful look as he reached up to squeeze her hand before turning back to Madison with gentle resignation in his eyes. "If you've got the time, Son, I'd like to take another look at those plans."

Chapter Twelve

Andrea's chest felt cold and empty as though her heart had plummeted through the floor, robbing her of speech, of thought, of feeling. Attempting to swallow, she felt as if her throat were glued shut. When she finally found her voice, it was hoarse and tremulous.

"There *has* to be a mistake, Mo. He just wouldn't. . . . Is there some way to verify this?" *Déjà-vu,* she thought wryly, remembering how she'd wrongly jumped to conclusions about him before.

"Didn't you hear me?" Mo chided, her tone cynical.

"I heard you!" she snapped.

"Lydia says it was signed by Madison McKee. What more do we need to know?"

"I still think we should check this out before we panic."

Mo shook her head sadly and huffed out a breath of exasperation. "Listen to yourself. Your sense of reason is out-to-lunch, if you ask me. Quit making excuses for him."

Ignoring Mo's remarks, Andrea rose on unsteady legs and walked to the desk where she snatched up the phone.

"I'm going to call Madison right now. I have to give him the chance to explain," she said, her voice cracking with emotion.

Mo laid a restraining hand on her arm. "Don't waste your time."

She suppressed the urge to weep. "I have to."

"What for?" Mo demanded. "He's just going to feed you more brilliant lies. If you can still believe he has good intentions, then he can make you believe anything. Wake up, Andie!" She sprang to her feet and grasped Andrea's shoulders. "I know you've fallen hard for this guy, but don't you see? He's as slick and as conniving and as evil as they come. He's been planning to tear this house down around my ears all along."

"I still think we should hear what he has to say," Andrea said quietly, refusing to allow herself to admit that Mo could be right.

"Ohhh! I give up." She threw her hands up in disgust. "Do what you want. Right now I've got to concentrate on this lunch party." She marched toward the door, then stopped and turned, shaking a finger in Andrea's direction. "But I'll tell you what. I'm not going to take it lying down. Madison McKee will be sorry he ever meddled with me." She stormed from the room, slamming the door behind her.

For a few seconds Andrea stood nursing her fractured feelings, then summoned up the strength to dial Madison's office.

It was almost a relief when the receptionist told her he was in a meeting and could not be disturbed. Good, she'd just as soon not have to hear a possible confirmation of the bad news. She needed time to soothe her charged emotions before confronting him. "Tell him it's Andrea Dusseaux and please have him call me as soon as he's out of the meeting."

She set the receiver down and leaned against the desk.

She knew she was probably deluding herself, but there *had* to be a rational, logical explanation.

But as the doubt slowly pushed its way to the forefront in her thoughts, she pressed a fist to her lips. Was Mo's accusation true? Was she herself so blinded by her desperate need for love, that she was manufacturing excuses for Madison's lies?

No, she reprimanded herself, remembering her promise not to doubt him again. She would withhold judgement until she'd heard his explanation. He deserved at least that. Anyone did.

She consciously focused her attention on the busy lunch crowd while making a deliberate effort to evade Mo who seemed fully occupied with the private party upstairs. Better avoid exacerbating the tension between them while she waited for Madison to get back to her.

When she hadn't heard from him by one o'clock, she marched to Mo's office to place a second call.

"He's gone to lunch," the chirpy receptionist announced matter-of-factly.

"This is Andrea Dusseaux again. I asked you to have him call me at the end of the meeting." She struggled to control the exasperation that tinged her voice.

"You probably spoke to Blanche. Mr. McKee must have gotten the message, because I see the copy here. I'm sure he will phone you the first chance he gets. I'll make a note that you called again."

"Thanks," Andrea muttered as she replaced the receiver and stared ahead blankly.

The sickening realization that it was a deliberate avoidance on his part struck her. She had to face the heart-wrenching truth that his professed love for her had been nothing more than a carefully calculated sham. And she'd fallen into his trap with her eyes wide open.

Anger settled in her stomach like cold lead, as the veil of his duplicity lifted from her eyes. He'd used her, endeared himself to Christopher . . . Was the trip to Sedona part of the deceit? Visions of their supreme intimacy in the fire tower came flooding in. Oh, God, how humiliating!

As the painful prospect sank into her mind, her attention was drawn to the calendar she'd been absently staring at. *Andrea back to New York*, Mo had scribbled under Friday, the 21st. Four days to go. Hadn't she done enough damage already? Not to mention alienating the only true friend she had in the world. An icy determination stiffened her spine as she reached for the phone. Why wait until Friday?

Drained of all emotion and moving mechanically like a robot in the cluttered bedroom, Andrea resolutely folded clothes into her suitcase. For the last two hours she'd see-sawed between white-hot anger and fathomless grief. She'd wept until there were no tears left to shed. It was vital to retain the desensitizing calm that now presided over her. To let go for one second would surely strike down her resolve.

She stiffened when she heard the front door slam and mentally braced herself for the confrontation.

"What are you doing?" Mo inquired breathlessly from the doorway.

"What does it look like I'm doing?" she replied, not looking up, realizing her eyes were red and swollen.

Mo sat on the edge of the bed and stared up into Andrea's face. "You've been crying! I'm sorry about what I said, kiddo," she said gently. "You know better than to take seriously all the garbage I mouth off."

"It's not what you said and I'm not angry with you."

"Then why are you packing?"

"Because my leaving today would be best for all concerned. I've made a colossal mess of everything, compromised your situation, not to mention what I've done to myself."

Mo sighed deeply. "I didn't mean all the things I said about Madison. I'm sure he has real feelings for you. Who in his right mind wouldn't? And maybe there *is* some kind of explanation."

"Nice try." Andrea threw her an affectionate smile, easily seeing through the transparent effort to cheer her up. "You can quit trying to soften the blow. My eyes are open now. And hopefully time will take care of the rest. Meanwhile, I'm getting out of your way, so you can handle the issue without me clouding it." She snapped her suitcase shut. "My flight leaves at five."

"Can't we talk about it?" Mo pleaded, taking both her hands.

"What for? You know I'm right."

"No, you're not. I've had time to cool off and think about everything since lunch. I'm the one who needed to open my eyes," she exclaimed fervently. "You tried to give me good advice and I ignored you."

Andrea drew away, puzzled. "Me? And what words of wisdom might those have been?"

"You know the difference between us? You always sell yourself short, and I'm so pig-headedly sure I'm right all the time. But you know something? I couldn't have been more wrong."

Andrea sighed and slumped wearily onto the bed beside her. "I haven't the foggiest idea what you're talking about."

Mo cast her a troubled look and chewed on her lower lip for a few seconds before rising to pace back and forth. "This whole condemnation thing could have been avoided if I'd accepted Russell Stanton's offer in the first place. But true to my usual self, I was too damn stubborn to see the writing on the wall."

"That doesn't excuse Madison."

"I'm not excusing him. He should have been up front

with us, but it's unfair to blame him for what happened. Stanton started it. Madison was just the hired gun.''

"What's your point, Mo?"

She stopped pacing and stared out the window. "It's funny. All this time I'd convinced myself that my fight to save Sundial House was for Christopher's benefit."

Andrea knotted her brows in surprise. "Isn't it?"

"No. I've been transferring my own insecurities into this issue. I've been so fiercely determined to make sure Christopher had the solid roots my dad never gave me, I deluded myself into believing that having a business and staying put in the same house represented security for him."

"I think you've done a wonderful job raising him alone. Don't you see, *you're* his security. Not things."

Mo gave her a long searching look. "That's not true either. Having a brain tumor was pretty sobering. What if I'd died? I'd have left a six-year-old a restaurant to run and a house that's falling apart, instead of a decent bundle of cash that would ensure his future?"

"If we'd had a crystal ball, we'd have both done things differently." Andrea couldn't suppress the sadness that welled up inside her again as she rose to hug her. They stood in silence, holding on to each other.

"Are you gonna be okay?" Mo asked drawing back.

"I'll survive. Maybe I'll follow your example and remain mateless. It's not worth the pain."

"Men are definitely the pits. Didn't you ever wonder why I never remarried?"

Andrea was glad to see a spark of humor return to Mo's eyes. "Because you could never find anybody crazy enough to put up with you," she said, allowing herself a rueful smile.

"Well, that's true enough," she said with a chuckle, then her expression grew serious. "The real reason is I figured if Christopher never had a father, he would never have a dad that would leave."

"What twisted bizarre logic," Andrea scoffed, then glanced at her watch. "I'd love to continue this fascinating conversation, but I've got to get going."

"I don't understand why you have to leave today. I *said* it's not your fault."

"You're going to have your hands full and I'd just as soon avoid a showdown with Madison."

Mo's eyes softened. "I didn't tell you this, but I sort of hoped things would work out between you two, and you'd decide to stay here and help me. Wouldn't that have been fabulous?"

"Wishful thinking, Mo."

With the amicable lunch now behind him, Madison felt a rush of elation after he'd escorted a smiling Russell Stanton to the elevator and returned to his office. *Yes! He'd done it,* he thought as he thrust a victorious fist in the air. He could hardly wait to share his triumph with Andrea. If his persuasive tactics were as successful with Maureen, he was home free. With all obstacles removed, he would no longer have to hold back. A smile played on his lips as he envisioned Andrea's reaction when he asked her to marry him.

He caught Blanche grinning at him from behind her desk, one brow cocked above her glasses, maternal pride shining from her eyes.

"It's going to be hard to come down to earth after pulling off a coup like that, but I don't suppose there is room in your state of euphoria for a small stack of mundane messages," she teased, waving the notes.

"The way I feel right now, Blanche, I can handle anything," he said, snatching the messages from her hand.

His blood was still racing as he returned to his office.

Although tempted to read his father the riot act for his interference—albeit well-meaning—which could have spoiled everything, he decided against any recriminations.

"You did your old man proud, Son. That was one hell of a presentation," McKee Sr. exclaimed with exaggerated enthusiasm.

"Thanks, but no thanks to you. What on earth possessed you to try and push that condemnation notice through without checking with me first?"

"Hey, the request was already in the file. I just got the ball rolling."

Madison shook his head. "Come on, Dad! You were sitting right there when Blanche brought me the file and you knew damn well I hadn't the time to study it before I left for Tucson. I didn't even know the request was in there."

"Wait a minute! *I* have a bone to pick with *you*. Why did you have to jump through hoops and complicate the situation for everybody just to save that old house? What was the point?"

"I have my reasons." He gave his father a sly smile.

McKee Sr.'s eyes widened. "Oh, I see. I should have guessed. You've gone and gotten yourself hung up on the Callaway woman."

"No, but you're on the right track. It's her friend, Andrea Dusseaux."

"How could you go and let yourself get side-tracked when you knew how important the outcome of this case was to me?"

Madison shrugged. "You don't plan these things. I saw her and fell in love. Have you forgotten how that feels?"

"I take it all back, Son. As usual, I was just thinking of myself," he said shame-faced while motioning for Madison to sit beside him. "I gather this must be pretty serious. Do you want to tell me about it?"

Madison eased himself next to his father and gave him

a brief overview, explaining how he and Andrea had started off on the wrong foot when they'd met, the strong feelings they had for each other and the dilemma he'd found himself in.

"So to answer your question, Dad, yes, it's serious enough that I plan to ask her to marry me."

McKee Sr. grabbed Madison's arm, a smile crinkling his face. "Congratulations, Son, she must be one special lady. Your mom will be tickled pink when she hears this." His exhuberance suddenly faded. "And I almost ruined it for you."

He suppressed a smile. "Yep, almost. Thank God we had the condemnation request withdrawn before word got out."

"Amen."

Madison was suddenly aware of the stack of messages in his hand. "I hate to kick you out, but it's almost four and I've got to return some of these calls, not to mention a certain important matter that needs to be wrapped up with Maureen Callaway," he said, giving him a pointed glance.

"I'm gone." McKee Sr. rose and moved to the door. "Good luck."

Sifting through the stack of messages as he hurried to his desk, Madison saw that Andrea had called twice. While elated that she'd phoned, he felt a touch of frustration that he hadn't known about it and had not returned the calls.

When he phoned the restaurant, he was told that Mo and Andrea were at home. Perfect, he decided, gathering up the presentation material. It would be helpful to have Andrea's support when he made his appeal.

Filled with anxious anticipation, he arrived at the little house in record time and bounded up the stairs.

The forbidding expression on Maureen's face when she opened the front door surprised him. "Hi," he began.

"If you have a few minutes, I'd like to talk with you and Andrea."

"You've got a lot of gall showing up on my doorstep."

Madison drew back, stung by her hostility. "I apologize for coming without an appointment, but I have something exceptional to tell you."

"I'll say it's exceptional. I got a call from a friend of mine this morning at City Planning. She filled me in on what you're up to."

He stared at her, feeling as though he'd been dealt a swift kick in the gut. "I'm sorry you had to hear about that. It was a miscommunication. I didn't know about it myself until this afternoon."

"Oh, really. Did another Madison McKee sign it?" she asked sarcastically.

"Yes. My father."

Maureen's eyes grew round with bewilderment, but a glint of suspicion still lurked despite his revelation.

"I understand fully why you're upset," he continued hastily. "I can explain everything if you'll permit me."

For a few awful seconds he thought she might refuse him, so he never let his gaze waver from hers and was relieved when she wordlessly waved him into the living room. She pointed him to the couch and then settled opposite him, her eyes still hard with skepticism.

Madison immediately launched into his proposal and gradually felt more at ease as he watched the indignation fade from her face.

"This is too overwhelming for me to fully grasp all at once," she said. "I need time to think."

"I don't expect you to make a decsion this minute, but you do see all the advantages?"

There was a flicker of humor behind her thoughtful gaze. "I was joking with Andie when I said you'd have to be a magician to resolve this, but I underestimated you." She cocked her head. "You really do love her, don't you."

"Was there ever a doubt?" Seeing the sudden alarm in Maureen's eyes sent a jolt of anxiety through him. "Oh no. Don't tell me she knows about the condemnation notice."

"I'm afraid so," she answered in a small voice.

He jumped up, a feeling of dread twisting in his stomach. "Where is she anyway?"

There was a look of total misery on Maureen's face. "Probably ready to board her flight to New York."

Andrea slumped back into the hard plastic chair in the crowded waiting area when she heard the announcement that her flight had been delayed yet another hour. She gave a feeble sigh, too spent to even feel frustration.

The initial anger at Madison was now a dull ache, hidden under thick layers of regret, sadness, desolation ... Her emotions were so entangled, so fused together, it was difficult to define any single one.

She pulled out the magazine she'd bought and tried to read, but the words blurred into meaningless text while nagging questions tortured her. How could she have misjudged his character so badly? Was she making the right decision leaving so suddenly, or should she have stayed to confront him, to release her anger and let it flame to the surface?

In all likelihood she would never see him again, and even though she knew now that would be the wisest course, it left a void in her as deep as an ocean.

Andrea tried to concentrate on the magazine, but in spite of her efforts to maintain a placid demeanor, to keep her emotions hidden from view, she was unable to shake the feeling that everyone was staring at her, judging her. "Fool!" they all seemed to be saying. "You gave your heart, body and soul to a man who was toying with you, using you!"

Why hadn't she been able to see through him? She

recalled the evening she'd found him with another woman at the club dining room. How glibly he'd explained it away. And as hard as she tried, she could not shake the memory of the magic of those hours she'd spent with him, the taste of his lips, the touch of his hands on her eager body. In two short weeks she had experienced both heaven and hell.

Suppressing the sob that rose to her throat, she wrenched her mind away from him only to have it replay the tearful good-bye with Mo and Christopher. With promises to write and call, she'd hugged the breath from Mo, and then squeezed Christopher to her. The feel of his small arms wrapped tightly around her neck renewed a sense of emptiness. How different her life would have been had she had a child to give her a reason to pick herself up, to go on.

She'd been misty-eyed when the cab had finally pulled up in front of the house.

"Are you sure you don't want me to drive you?" Mo had asked, her voice trembling.

"One agonizing good-bye is enough," she'd said adamantly, as she climbed into the taxi.

Andrea looked sadly at the airline ticket nestled inside the pocket of her jacket which lay across her lap. She'd come full circle during her brief stay in Phoenix, arriving disillusioned, but hopeful. And now . . . was she still hopeful? The dreary thought of returning to New York, to her barren, bland life, pressed like a heavy weight on her chest.

Enough regrets! She'd overcome losing her family, overcome so many obstacles, even Bernard. She was a survivor, she told herself as she inhaled deeply and sat tall in her chair. Lowering a soothing curtain over the painful thoughts, she idly watched her fellow travellers.

She jumped when she felt a hand on her shoulder and swung around to face Madison's penetrating gaze. "As much as I've chased you these past two weeks, I feel like

I could qualify for the Boston Marathon," he said with mock irritation.

Her heart seemed to stop beating, her lungs were devoid of oxygen. In the space of a few seconds, her fragile emotions soared to the sky, then plummeted back to earth.

"What are you doing here?" she asked wearily.

"Looking for you."

She watched him move around the row of seats and plant himself directly in front of her. Against her will she felt warm with pleasure that he'd come, but quickly stiffened her resolve. "Haven't you done enough already?"

"Did you really think you could get away from me so easily?"

Andrea felt too exhausted and detached to even muster up any anger. "Leave me alone."

"Not until you listen to me." He obstinately folded his arms, indicating that he planned to stay.

Aware that the people nearby were staring at them, she threw him a defiant glare. "Are you going to cause a scene right here?"

He arched a brow in challenge. "If that's what it takes. Are you going to let me explain?"

"You should be doing your explaining to Mo."

"I just did," he said breaking into a grin. "How else would I know you were here?"

"She told you?" Andrea asked incredulously.

"Yes."

Andrea's mind whirled with confusion.

"Why don't you sit down here, young man," the woman beside her offered, gathering up her knitting and sliding into the next chair, a shrewd twinkle gleaming in her watery green eyes as she glanced back and forth between them.

"Thank you, Ma'am," he said, jumping at the offer.

Andrea shifted uncomfortably when he sat beside her. His close proximity set her raw nerves on edge.

"The last thing I want to do is quarrel with you, Andie,"

he said softly. She looked like a frightened dove poised for flight and he ached to hold her. "All I ask is five minutes to clear up this misunderstanding. Then if you still want me to leave, I will."

"Fair enough," she said, folding her hands tightly in her lap. She at least owed him that much.

Madison felt his insides trembling. It had been difficult enough convincing Russ and Maureen, but it was imperative that he now deliver the finest summation of his life.

He watched anxiously for her reaction as he launched into a full explanation of what had occurred and was elated to see the dark look of cynicsm begin to fade from her turquoise eyes. She was silent when he finished.

"So far I've managed to please everybody but you." He took her hand in his. "Please don't leave today."

Andrea gave him a searching look as she struggled with the conflict that churned inside her. "I have to."

His heart plunged in dismay. The notion of losing her was unthinkable. "Why? You told me last week there was nothing to keep you in New York."

She couldn't think of an answer that made sense.

Madison cupped her chin in his hand. "Can you look into my eyes and tell me you don't love me?"

She let out a shuddery sigh. "You know I can't, but staying isn't the answer." She gave him a beseeching look. "Don't you see? I mistrusted you again when I promised myself I wouldn't. I convicted you before you had an opportunity to defend yourself."

"It's all right," he said tenderly. "I understand."

"No, you don't." She turned her head away. "I can't seem to break the pattern. It may sound crazy but I'm afraid if I allow myself to love people, I'll lose them." She met his eyes again. "Maybe I need to see a shrink."

"You don't need a shrink," he murmured, leaning forward to kiss the end of her nose. "I already have the perfect cure."

She glanced around shyly, wondering what everyone around them must think. "I hesitate to ask what that might be."

"All you need is Dr. McKee's special prescription, which is my pledge to love you for the rest of our lives," he said, bringing his lips to hers. Their kiss was long and deep as they clung to each other. She reluctantly pulled away, barely hearing the announcement from the loudspeaker. "That's my flight."

"Not any more, it isn't."

"But ... my bags ... they're already on the plane! All my clothes ..."

He intercepted her words with another kiss then whispered in her ear. "Where we're going, you won't need any."

Spent and basking in the afterglow of their passion, Andrea lavished Madison's shoulder with soft kisses and uttered a satisfied sigh. She fluffed the heart-shaped pillow behind her back and stretched her arm out languidly to admire the diamond wedding ring on her finger. Its luster rivaled the glitter of the Las Vegas Strip outside their hotel window.

"Mrs. Madison McKee, Jr.," she said softly, a smile curling her lips. "Yes, I like the sound of that."

Madison turned and snuggled his face between her breasts. "Mmmmm. Me too." He slid down to rest his head on her thigh, then looked up at her with an impish grin. "I feel the urge to start on another generation of McKees right now."

Her eyes widened in disbelief. "Now?"

He reached for her. "It's as good a time as any."

AS AN INTRODUCTION TO
SYLVIA NOBEL'S AWARD-WINNING
KENDALL O'DELL MYSTERY SERIES
WE INVITE YOU TO PREVIEW
THE FOLLOWING BONUS CHAPTERS

In

DEADLY SANCTUARY

CONTINUE TO FOLLOW THE
SUSPENSE-PACKED
ADVENTURES OF FEISTY,
FLAME-HAIRED REPORTER
KENDALL O'DELL

IN

THE DEVIL'S CRADLE
DARK MOON CROSSING
SEEDS OF VENGEANCE

Published by
Nite Owl Books
Phoenix, Arizona

WE INVITE YOU TO READ THE FIRST
CHAPTER OF EACH BOOK POSTED ON OUR
WEBSITE AT: WWW.NITEOWLBOOKS.COM

Print and e-Books are available through most retail book outlets and
online bookstores.

SYLVIA NOBEL

DEADLY SANCTUARY

Chapter One

"Oh...my...God. What have I done?" I murmured aloud, staring transfixed at the barren desert valley below the roadside overlook. No way could this be my new home. No way. As I consulted the Arizona road map once again, a hostile brown wind charged up the steep cliff, whirling my hair into a tangle and filling my eyes with grit.

I began to regret my impulsive decision to take the newspaper job in Castle Valley. But, had there been any choice? All through the drive from Pennsylvania I had tortured myself with 'If onlys.' If only I hadn't been forced to a drier climate because of asthma. If only I hadn't lost my job at the Philadelphia Inquirer. If only Grant hadn't dumped me. If only, if only...

An odd smell and snuffling sound made me whirl around. Instantly, I froze in shock at the sight of eight weird-looking creatures approximately the size of large dogs standing between me and the safety of my car.

A tentative step forward caused one of the grayish, bristle-coated animals to let out a snort and clatter its long, sharp tusks. What the devil were these things? They looked ferocious, like something out of a science fiction movie. Heart hammering, I shrank back against the stone retaining wall and edged a glance behind me to the sheer drop. There was no escape unless I suddenly developed the ability to fly.

A surge of panic contracted my chest. Stay calm, I urged myself. The last thing I needed right now was an asthma attack and to make matters worse, I realized that I'd left my inhaler in the car. If only a balky fuel pump hadn't detoured me off the freeway to Prescott for repairs, I wouldn't have even been in this godforsaken spot.

For whatever reason, the strange beasts suddenly lost interest in me. They dipped their heads and rooted among the dry weeds, flicking only an occasional wary look at me. I wondered what else I could do to screw up my life.

As I stood baking in the warm April sunlight, I cringed inwardly remembering how my well-meaning father had oversold my abilities to his old newspaper colleague Morton Tuggs, convincing him that I was already an experienced investigative reporter.

"Dad!" I'd whispered fiercely, "You know I was only in research."

He'd cupped his hand over the receiver. "It's not like you have a lot of options, Kendall. This place isn't far from Phoenix and he's got an opening right now. You talk to him." He set the phone against my ear.

After I'd introduced myself, he explained that not only would my investigative background be a plus, he also needed someone he could trust. Three weeks prior, he stated, one of his reporters had mysteriously vanished without a trace.

That snagged my interest, but I felt a vague sense of foreboding when he seemed reluctant to answer any further questions on the phone.

"If you decide to take the job," he'd added gruffly, "we'll talk more when you arrive."

That would have been the time to confess my amateur status, but I'd said nothing.

The sound of an approaching vehicle pulled my attention to the road and a surge of relief washed over me when a tan pickup pulling a horse trailer roared into view. I waved my hand and the truck eased to a stop on the far side of the road. Two men got out. The driver, a tall lanky man wearing mirrored sunglasses, strolled toward me then stopped in his tracks and stared.

His older companion limped up behind him and gestured to my Volvo. "You got car trouble?"

I shook my head and pointed. Both men peered around the car, looked back at me, at each other, then broke into wide grins.

"Those pigs botherin' you, lady?" asked the tall one, tipping the hat off his forehead, his mouth working a piece of gum. There was an unmistakable note of sarcasm in his voice.

Pigs? These hairy, sharp-toothed things were pigs? But why should that surprise me? They were like everything else I'd seen so far in this hot, dusty place: wild, prickly, and ugly.

He stepped forward, clapped his hands, and hollered, "Eeeeyaah!" The animals squealed and galloped away.

He turned back to me and swept the wide brimmed western hat from his head, revealing thick, blue-black hair. With exaggerated flair, he executed an elaborate bow, his smile mocking. "Always happy to assist a damsel in distress." Even though I couldn't see his eyes, I could tell by the slow movement of his head that he was eyeing me from head to foot.

Damsel? Great. Was that how I appeared? Weak? Helpless? I squared my jaw, not sure if it was his macho behavior that irked me, or the fact that I was thoroughly fed up with men at that particular moment. A failed marriage and a broken engagement certainly entitled me to that.

The older man explained that the creatures weren't actually pigs but Collared Peccaries called javelinas. "They look a mite fearsome, but won't usually harm you unless you go after their young'uns." A friendly smile creased his sun-leathered face. By the look of their clothing, I gathered I'd come across some genuine Arizona cowboys.

"Should have guessed," the tall stranger said scornfully, pointing to my license plate. "She's a bird."

I bristled. "What do you mean I'm a bird?"

"Snowbird," the other man explained. "You know, tourist. Winter visitor. Folks who come here for the warm weather and then skedaddle."

"But," the contentious one cut in, "not before you interlopers pollute our air, clog our roads, drain our water supply and ruin our way of life."

"No offense intended, ma'am." The old cowboy shot a questioning glance at his friend.

But I did feel offended. Without stopping to think, the lie leaped to my tongue. "I am not a snowbird. For your information, I happen to be relocating to Castle Valley. I've accepted a very important...managerial position at their newspaper." I regretted my impulsive words immediately and wondered why I should even give a crap what this arrogant man thought.

For a long minute they stared at me in silence, and then the tall cowboy grinned. "Well, now, is that a fact?"

A sharp ringing sound like metal striking metal, and a high whinny from the trailer got both men's immediate attention. "Come on, Jake," said the younger man, "we've wasted enough time. Let's get them back to the ranch." He reached the trailer in long strides, and I could hear him speak in a soothing voice to the horses.

I thanked Jake for his help, adding, "I'm not too crazy about your friend. He's got a real attitude problem."

His grin seemed rather sheepish. "Don't pay no attention to him. He just don't like newcomers much, and plus that you look a powerful lot like..."

His words faded as the ground suddenly swirled beneath me. I brushed a hand over my forehead as Jake stepped forward. Grabbing one arm, he led me to sit on a nearby rock in the shade of a scraggly tree. "You got water with you, miss?" A look of concern deepened the creases around his eyes. "It's real dangerous to be out here without some. People dehydrate in a matter of hours. The desert, it ain't nothing to fool with."

I decided I'd rather die than admit I was an ignorant snowbird. "Yes, I have plenty in the car." He didn't need to know I had only a few sips of soda left in my cup.

A loud shout from the truck. "Come on, Jake. Let's roll!"

I thanked Jake again for his kindness. He touched the brim of his hat murmuring, "Don't mention it," and limped away.

The dizzy spell behind me, I slumped into the oven-like interior of my car and downed the last of the warm soda, jumping in alarm when a hand reached through the window on the passenger side.

The dark-haired man dropped a thermos on the seat beside me. "You might need this."

I glared at him. "I'm perfectly fine. And anyway, I would have no way of returning this to you since it's highly unlikely we'll ever meet again." The haughty tone in my voice surprised me.

His slow grin was downright sardonic. "It's a small world. You never know." Waving a final salute in my direction, he headed back to the truck. I felt like he'd given me the finger as they pulled away. His bumper sticker read, WELCOME TO ARIZONA. NOW GO HOME!

By the time I reached the sign informing me that Castle Valley was fifteen miles ahead, I'd drunk half the water and was feeling rather foolish. The cowboy had been right after all.

Slowing for a cattle guard, I noticed a girl walking alongside the road. It wasn't my usual habit to stop for hitchhikers, but when she frantically shouted and waved, I pulled onto the shoulder. She begged for a ride and when I reluctantly agreed, she scooped up her backpack and plopped down beside me, exclaiming. "It's hotter than hell out here." I agreed and tried not to notice that she hadn't been within whistling distance of a shower for some time. "You going to Phoenix?" she asked hopefully.

"No. Just to the next town."

"Oh." A look of resignation flickered across her thin face. "No biggie. I'll get another ride. You mind if I smoke?" She flipped a damp blond curl behind one ear.

"Yeah, I mind," I answered, trying not to stare at the multitude of tattoos adorning her body, the studs in her nose, eyebrows, and that her ears must have been pierced a hundred times. Every time she moved, the array of earrings jingled when she moved.

"That's cool. No problem." There was a hard edge about her. I noted her ragged jeans and faded T-shirt. What in the world was this girl doing out here in the middle of nowhere? Was she a runaway? She couldn't be more than fourteen. As we continued down the road, she spoke little, staring straight ahead with vacant green eyes.

I dragged my thoughts from the girl to examine my new surroundings. Morton Tuggs had told my father that Castle Valley was a beautiful place and more healthful than Phoenix for me because it had no smog and was higher in elevation. My initial reaction was one of extreme disappointment. What a dinky town. It looked old and dilapidated, not at all what I'd imagined. A sign read: Population 5000. I wondered if that included the wildlife as a prairie dog skipped across the road in front of me.

At least the sunset was gorgeous. The sky boasted a brilliant tapestry of red, yellow and orange hues, tinting the rock wall to the east a vibrant shade of gold.

I stopped near the Greyhound Bus station, pressed a twenty-dollar bill into the girl's hand and suggested there might be a church or shelter where she could spend the night. She thanked me and got out, saying that the money would come in handy since she was headed for Texas. As I watched her walk away I suddenly felt very fortunate. Unlike her, I'd be staying at a motel tonight and I had a new job waiting for me in the morning.

I slept like a rock and rose late. As I downed my asthma medication, I prayed that the dry weather would restore my health and then I could return home.

When I arrived at the address I'd been given, my spirits
tanked. How was I going to survive in this place? The
newspaper building looked just like the rest of the downtown
area - old and weather-beaten.

The receptionist at the Castle Valley Sun greeted me with a
dimpled smile, and introduced herself as Ginger King. She
seemed delighted to hear that I might be joining the staff and
took my elbow in a friendly manner while ushering me to
Morton Tuggs' office, which was situated at the end of a short L-
shaped hallway.

I couldn't help but notice the smudged walls and frayed
carpet as we reached the open doorway. From inside, a loud
voice boomed, "The hell you say?" Hesitating, I turned
questioning eyes to Ginger. "Don't fret none, sugar pie," she
soothed, patting my hand. "His bark's a mite worse than his bite.
You can set right there in front of his desk." Giggling, she gave
me a little shove forward. The bald, red-faced man seated at the
incredibly cluttered desk waved me in while continuing to
harangue whomever was at the other end of the phone.

The wooden chair wobbled on uneven legs when I sat.
Clutching my purse in my lap, I surveyed the room. It was
crowded and shabby, relieved only by bright travel posters
plastered on every available square inch of wall space.

"I paid you a shitload of money for this goddamned
system," he shouted. He didn't have hair one on the crown of his
head, but as he listened intently, his fingers absently fluffed, then
pressed flat, the tufts of fuzz perched over his ears like gray
cotton balls. "I don't give a rat's ass what you say, just get the
hell over here and fix it!" The phone dinged when he slammed
down the receiver.

After a few breaths to compose himself he edged me an
apologetic smile. "Sorry about that." He reached out a
welcoming hand. "So, you're Kendall O'Dell? Good to meet you.
I see you got Bill's red hair. Quite a guy your dad. I guess he told
you the story?" His brown eyes looked solemn, faraway. I took
his hand, knowing he must be remembering the day my dad had

saved his life when they'd both been foreign correspondents during the Vietnam War.

"It's nice to finally meet you too, Mr. Tuggs."

His other hand swiped impatiently at the air. "Tugg. Tugg. Everybody calls me Tugg." A hint of humor lit his face. "Except when they're calling me Tugboat behind my back."

I smiled, finally relaxing. We talked for a few minutes about what my routine assignments would be, the fact that his wife Mary had located several houses for me to look at and other general subjects.

During a lull in the conversation, I shifted uncomfortably in my chair. Was I wrong, or was Morton Tuggs deliberately avoiding the subject I most wanted to discuss? I cleared my throat. "You said on the phone you needed someone with my investigative background and someone you could trust. Do you want to tell me about this missing reporter?"

A look of anxiety etched his face. Instead of answering, he rose, shut the door, and returned to his desk where he laced his fingers in front of him. "I have to tell you that I've agonized for several weeks over how to handle this. It was my intent to have you look into it but, under the circumstances...perhaps it would be best not to pursue the matter further."

I eyed him suspiciously. He wasn't behaving very much like the hard-boiled newspaper editor my father had described. "A man doesn't vanish for no reason. What did the police report say?"

"There was a search. It was called off last week. I've pressed, but there doesn't seem much interest in pursuing the case. The official line coming down is that he probably just got bored with our little burg and skipped."

"What do you think?"

Tugg absentmindedly fluffed the patches of hair again. "John Dexter wasn't real well liked. He delighted in digging up dirt on people. Go through some of the back issues and you'll see what I mean. He had a knack for really pissing people off. But,"

he added, "even though he was sort of flaky at times, I can't
believe he'd just up and go with no notice."

"So, I'll talk to the police and see what I can come up with.
Perhaps there's a lead they've missed."

"No!"

I jumped as his fist crashed on the desk. Then, noting my
obvious shock, he said, "I'm sorry. I didn't mean to startle
you...it's just that...I'm not sure giving you this assignment would
be the right thing to do."

Butterflies fluttered in my stomach. The major reason for
my trip, resurrecting my aborted career, was fading before my
eyes. "I'd appreciate a shot at this."

He swiveled in his chair and stared silently at the poster of
Greece. After a minute he said quietly, "If you decide to work on
this, it'll have to be strictly on the Q.T. Nobody else can know,
and I'd caution you to be very, very careful."

His attitude disturbed me. It wasn't what he was saying, it
was what he wasn't saying.

"Mr. Tuggs, Tugg..." I tried to keep the irritation from my
voice. "You're going to have to level with me on this or I don't
see how I can help. If you suspect foul play, which I gather you
do, why aren't the police pursuing it, and why aren't you pushing
for answers?"

As if struggling mightily with a difficult decision, he
dropped his eyes and drummed his fingers on the arm of his
chair. Abruptly, he pulled open a drawer and extracted a ragged
piece of paper. He stared at it, chewing his lower lip. "John
called me at home the afternoon before he disappeared. We were
having a big get-together for my daughter and it was so noisy I
was having trouble hearing him. I wish now I'd paid more
attention 'cause I only remember bits and pieces of what he
said." He sighed heavily. "Something about meeting a girl later.
Her information would tie into what he'd been working on
earlier in the week, and if he was right, it would blow the lid off
this town." He stopped, rubbed his temples as if in pain, then
continued. "He'd been going through some files over at the

sheriff's office and told me he'd discovered something weird. I'm not sure if there's any connection, but, I found this in his desk a couple of days ago."

I studied the smudged paper he handed me. In between a profusion of doodling, I read the scattered phrases: Med records gone. Both cases. Dead teens. T prof...Connection? Possible cover up?

Before I could speak he added, "One more thing. And, this is a doozy, the part that's really got me boxed into a corner. The last thing he said before he hung up was, "'Whatever you do, don't mention this to Roy.'"

I looked up. "Who's Roy?"

The pained expression again. "My goddamned brother-in-law."

It was frustrating having to drag every word from him. "So?"

"He owns half this newspaper and...he's the sheriff."

Chapter Two

I left Morton Tuggs' office, my head still reeling from his disturbing revelations, and trotted after Ginger, who'd been charged with familiarizing me with the layout. For the moment, I pushed the John Dexter puzzle to the back of my mind.

In the paper-littered production room, I shook hands with Harry, a big, burly man with coffee stains on his T-shirt, and then Rick, who peered at me owlishly through thick, horn-rimmed glasses. Lupe and Al, busy on the phones with classifieds, flashed preoccupied smiles. While Ginger prattled on, filling my head with endless personal statistics about each employee, I strained to maintain an expression of interest. The place was much smaller than I had imagined.

"And this here's your office." She gave a grand sweep of her hand.

Inwardly, I cringed in dismay at the sight of the dingy room crammed with several filing cabinets and three scarred desks topped with piles of clutter. Two smeary windows faced east overlooking the parking lot.

"Jim's out on assignment, but I see Tally's still here. He writes all the sports goodies." She nodded toward a man hunched over a desk in the far corner with his back to us, the phone cradled on his shoulder. A playful lilt edged her words as she sang out, "Hey, darlin'! Turn 'round here and say 'howdy' to your new roommate."

Apparently absorbed on the phone, he didn't acknowledge us, so I told Ginger I'd meet him later. No sooner were the words spoken when he swiveled his chair around and stood to face us. Our eyes met, and my mouth sagged open as a jolt of recognition shot through me. It couldn't be! There in front of me clad in boots, jeans, and a checkered shirt, stood the tall, lanky cowboy from yesterday. The pig chaser.

He nodded. "Bradley Talverson at your service...again, ma'am." His lips twisted in a wry smile as he motioned toward a tiny, metal desk. "I hope you'll find the...ah...accommodations here in the executive office to your liking."

With a chill of embarrassment, I remembered my fabricated tale of an important managerial position. So, that's why he'd acted the way he had. He must have thought I was a complete ass and I had no doubt my face was as red as it felt. The expression in his dark eyes challenged me to react. For what seemed an eternity, I wrestled with disbelief, regret and irritation. There seemed only one right thing to do. I laughed.

A look of surprise flitted over his lean face. "Well," he chuckled, widening his stance and folding his arms across his chest. "I'm glad to see you have a sense of humor."

Ginger regarded the two of us with astonishment. "Y'all know each other?"

"In a manner of speaking," he told her, and I couldn't help but notice his eyes brushing over me again. We parted on a handshake and my promise to return his thermos in the morning.

As I moved to the front door, I could tell by the look on Ginger's face that she was dying to know how we'd met. But I'd have to tell her some other time. Tugg had arranged for me to meet his wife, Mary at her realty office, and I was already late.

En route to the address, I thought about the rest of my conversation with Tugg. The newspaper had been owned by his wife's family for many years and her father had been editor up until four years ago when ill health forced him to retire. Under pressure, Tugg had given up a good position at the Arizona Republic in Phoenix and relocated to Castle Valley. He'd found the Sun in sorry shape and deeply in debt. A large infusion of cash was needed to keep it afloat, but no lending institutions were interested. Help had finally come from within the family. Roy Hollingsworth, recently married to Mary's twin sister, Faye, had advanced the money.

"You can see why I haven't been able to pursue this myself," Tugg had said glumly. "I'm between that rock and hard place you always hear about. Can you imagine what would happen if the paper accused Roy of dragging his feet on this investigation? If he pulls his financial support, we're sunk, not to mention that Mary would probably divorce me."

I asked him the best way to approach the subject with his brother-in-law.

"With caution," he warned. "Roy's not a man to piss off. He's got a hard head, a short temper, and," Tugg emphasized with a scowl, "he carries a gun. Just remember that." Ushering me toward the door, he'd apologized for placing me in such a delicate spot, but felt with my background I'd be able to dig up something without being discovered. Once again, the opportunity had come for me to declare my amateur status, and, as before, I thought better of it.

"Why don't you just hire a private detective or something? That way there'd be no tie to the newspaper."

He looked weary. "I'm barely collecting a salary now. Where would I get fifty bucks an hour to hire one?"

As I parked the car at the Castle Valley Realty office, I had more than a few misgivings about my decision to accept the position.

Mary Tuggs welcomed me with a beaming smile as I stepped inside her office. "I'm so very glad to meet you."

At five foot eight, I towered over her tiny, round frame. "My goodness, aren't you a sight! You remind me of a young Katharine Hepburn. Do you know who she was?"

I did. That clinched it. I decided I liked Mary Tuggs a lot. Outside again, I wondered if she'd need a leg up as we approached her red Bronco. Somehow she scrambled into the

driver's seat without assistance. She showed me several
unremarkable dwellings nearby, renting for astronomical prices,
and then, noting my dismay, suggested a place located five miles
north of town. "Morty thought you might like to at least look at
it," she said, swinging onto the main highway. "But I'm not sure
you'll want to be so far from town."

She told me that the three-bedroom, two bath house was
vacant because the elderly owner, Teresa Delgado, was in a
Phoenix nursing home recovering from a fall. Afraid of
vandalism, she wanted Mary to find a trustworthy renter to
occupy it until she returned. "It's been empty for a month now,
so she's lowered the rent to get someone in there," she added.

"Sounds interesting," I replied, watching the cactus -covered
landscape fly past. There wasn't another house in sight when we
turned east and bounced along a rutted dirt road, leaving a plume
of swirling dust in our wake.

"This is Lost Canyon Road," Mary informed me. "You'll be
quite close to the Castle."

"Castle?"

She laughed and rolled her eyes. "Silly me. Of course you
wouldn't know yet. That's Castle Rock," she said, pointing
toward a mammoth, multi-colored rock formation. "It was
named 'Castillo del Viento' by Spanish settlers. It means castle
of the wind, isn't that pretty?"

I agreed and we'd just dipped into a dry sandy riverbed she
called a 'wash' and were rounding a turn on the opposite hill,
when she suddenly wrenched the wheel to the right. A black
Mercedes with heavily tinted windows roared by leaving us in a
choking cloud of dust.

My heart racing madly, I wheezed and reached for my
inhaler.

"I'm so sorry!" White-faced, she pressed one hand to her
chest. "What a maniac. He didn't even slow down." She shoved
the truck into gear, grumbling, "That had to be someone from
Serenity House. Except for the Hinkle Ranch a couple miles
south of Tess's place, no one else lives out this way."

I took a few deep breaths and let the medication seep slowly into my lungs. "What's Serenity House?"

She slanted me a sidelong glance. "Well...it's a mental hospital."

That captured my attention. "No kidding? What's it doing out here in the middle of the desert?"

"The property was cheap. It's on the site of an old Spanish monastery which was crumbling to ruins. Some developer restored it and tried to make a go of it as a health spa. When that failed, a psychiatrist named Isadore Price bought it about six years ago." She pursed her lips into a thin line. "That was probably his Mercedes."

"I hope he's a better doctor than he is a driver." Mary frowned. "He's kind of a peculiar old bird. Keeps to himself mostly. I've only seen him a few times in town at a couple of social gatherings."

"Have there ever been any problems at this place?"

"To be honest, there was an incident right after they opened. One of the male patients escaped. He'd chopped up his family or something."

I shivered involuntarily.

"This town's never seen such excitement!" Her face became animated at the memory. "There was a huge manhunt, and everyone was pretty much on pins and needles until they found him. After that, a real high fence was built, and from what I've heard it's very well guarded. Nothing else has ever happened."

"How far is it from the Delgado place?"

"Less than two miles. And, of course, that's the whole idea of having it so secluded." She glanced at me again. "If it bothers you, I can turn around right now."

"No. I'd still like to see it."

"Okay," she said, steering onto another dirt road named Pajaro del Suspiro. Explaining it was Spanish for 'Weeping Bird,' she braked the truck in front of a brick-red ranch-style wooden house surrounded by golden palo verde trees and stands of saguaro cactus.

I got out and took a sniff of the warm, pristine air. Yep. Just what the doctor ordered. I followed Mary up the stone walkway and when she pointed to the giant rock formation, I stopped in amazement. It did resemble a castle and the effect was breathtaking.

While she fiddled with the door key, I listened to the lonesome keening of the wind and wondered if I could stand to live in such isolation. My misgivings faded as she led me through the spacious interior, decorated in bright Southwestern colors and heavy, Spanish-style furniture. It was a gigantic improvement over the cramped apartment I'd just left in Philadelphia, and far cheaper. I expressed surprise that she'd had difficulty keeping it rented.

"The trouble is," Mary said, showing me through the sunny kitchen, "most renters want a signed lease, and Tess won't have it because she wants the freedom to return on short notice. That's the minus, but," she added with a cheery smile, "here's a plus. The last tenants left in such a hurry, I never got a chance to refund their deposit. So, if you decide to take it, the first month would be free."

"I like the free part, but, what does the 'left in a hurry' part mean?"

Mary opened the front door. "They called me out of the blue late one night, and announced they were leaving right then and there."

"Why?"

There was no mistaking her tone of skepticism. "Tess certainly never mentioned it, but...they swore this place was haunted."

Chapter Three

Fascinated by Mary's intriguing remark, I chose to put aside my misgivings and move in. The proliferation of insects that trooped in and out of the Delgado house the first few days bothered me more than the supposed phantom. I'd always considered myself fairly brave for a woman, having no particular fear of snakes, mice, or bats. But, when it came to insects, spiders especially, I turned into a shivering coward. There seemed to be an abundance of the eight legged creatures about, plus scorpions, centipedes, and humongous roaches. At my request, Mary sent the exterminator.

On his second visit in three days, overall clad, grizzle-faced, Lloyd "Skeeter" Jenkins of the Bugs-Be-Gone Exterminating Company, told me all I needed to know, and more, about the insects and rodents indigenous to the great state of Arizona.

"Now I kin git rid o' them pesky mice fer ya, an'the powder I'll lay down'll keep them centipedes and scorpions on their toes, so to speak. Spiders is something else again. Them suckers kin walk right over the stuff with them long legs o' theirs."

He left me with the sage advice to "never put yer shoes on in the mornin' til you've whopped 'em good. There's no tellin' what kinda critter mighta moved in an' set up housekeepin' durin' the night."

I wondered if I'd ever get used to the bugs, the dust, and the scalding sun. The calendar said it was still April but I could have sworn spring had been canceled and we'd gone right into summer as it was already in the 90's. My asthma had improved, but I was miserably hot.

"Don't you worry, sugar," Ginger had soothed hearing my complaint, "as soon as your blood thins, you'll get used to it." I wasn't sure I wanted my blood to thin.

My first week on the job was an exercise in frustration and adaptation. The Sun, a sixteen page tabloid, was published only twice weekly, Wednesdays and Saturdays. I sorely missed the daily deadlines, the lively newsroom chatter, and stimulation of the big city. I knew I couldn't go back to damp, cool Pennsylvania and face a life of being incapacitated, yet I didn't want to stay either.

My other co-worker - young, blond, brash and not overly bright Jim Sykes - didn't sympathize with my position. He grabbed all the interesting assignments while I got the leftovers. If I had to cover one more banquet, Ladies Club function, or write one more article about who was visiting whom from out of town, I felt I'd go nuts.

After banging my knee on the narrow desk for the third time that morning, I grumbled, "I hate this damn thing."

Bradley Talverson swiveled around at my remark, and taunted me with a crooked grin. "Welcome to the club. We all started at the rookie desk. Now it's your turn."

"Yeah," young Sykes joined in. "Now that Johnny boy's split, you're low man on the totem pole."

I glanced swiftly from one to the other. Neither man seemed particularly disturbed by his disappearance, and I reminded myself again that even they could not know of my secret assignment. I phrased my question carefully, trying to sound indifferent. "Oh, yeah. What was he like? John Dexter, I mean?"

Bradley's eyes narrowed. "All hat and no cattle."

I raised an eyebrow. "Come again?"

"He was a pain in the ass. Interested only in trash journalism."

"But he was real popular with the ladies. Married or single, right Tally?" Jim's eyes gleamed wickedly.

I knew there was some significance to the remark by the deadly expression on Bradley's face before he turned his back to us. His constant mood swings puzzled me. Sometimes he was cordial and friendly. At other times, withdrawn, angry almost, as if he were struggling with some inner demon. More than once, I'd caught him looking at me with an unreadable expression in his dark eyes.

Anxious to pursue the subject of John Dexter, I had just formulated my next question when Ginger stuck her head in the doorway. "Come on, sugar, let's shake it. Time for lunch."

Damn! If only she had waited five minutes. Bradley and Jim resumed their work; my chance for more questions gone for now.

As we walked the three blocks to the Iron Skillet, I silently thanked God for Ginger King who'd unabashedly inserted herself into the vacant slot in my life marked: friend. Short and round with light brown hair and sparkling ginger-colored eyes, she bubbled over with good humor. She was also a hopeless gossip. Endearing, but hopeless.

Three days earlier, during our first lunch together, she'd shrieked with laughter when I recounted my story of meeting Bradley, whose close friends called him Tally, she informed me. I learned all about her family, that she'd been born in Georgia, relocated to Texas when she was fourteen, then to Arizona and finally her heartfelt desire to settle down and have children.

"How old are you, sugar?"

"Twenty-eight."

"Well, you still have some time. I'm gonna be thirty-three next month and eligible men in this town are scarcer than hen's teeth."

Mingled between anecdotes about the good citizens of Castle Valley, she skillfully extracted large chunks of my background.

"I got married right after college, but it lasted barely two years."

"Oh, that's a shame." For a few seconds her expression was sympathetic, then it turned impish. "So, what happened? He beat ya? Chase other women? Was he gay?"

I laughed. "I think you've been watching too many talk shows. Sorry to disappoint you, but it was nothing so dramatic. I'd been working at my dad's newspaper since I could read and could do every job there practically in my sleep.

I was restless, ready to move on and my husband was studying to be a pharmacist. His plans included us staying in Spring Hill, complete with picket fence and a dozen kids. Mine didn't. Neither of us could change, so we parted friends. He got the dog, and I took my maiden name back."

Throughout the remainder of the meal, she'd pressed me for further details, and it was amusing to hear some of the things I'd told her, repeated by other staff members the following day. Some details were embellished almost beyond recognition.

With that in mind now, as we entered the restaurant and slid into the red vinyl booth, I vowed to talk less of myself and concentrate on extracting information from her.

"Oh, lookee here," she cried, eyeing the menu with regret. "Chicken and dumplin's. And me on a stupid diet again."

"Go ahead and have it if you want it."

She drew back in mock horror. "Easy for you to say, being skinny as a rail. Food don't go to my stomach, darlin'. Everything goes right here," she complained, patting her hips.

We were both giggling when a chestnut-haired woman interrupted, asking for our order. "Oh, Lucy," Ginger gushed, a sly expression stealing over her features, "this is Kendall O'Dell. Kendall, this is Lucinda Johns. She and her Aunt Polly run this place."

When I told her how much I'd enjoyed the previous lunch, she smiled and thanked me. As she took our orders, I couldn't help but notice her enormous boobs. It made me feel positively flat.

"Kendall's our new gal on the beat over at the paper. Ain't that nice?" The syrupy tone of Ginger's voice surprised me.

Curious, I glanced at her, then back to Lucinda in time to see her smile shrink. "I see. Congratulations." She cast a speculative glance at me before turning away.

A mischievous light gleamed in Ginger's eyes. "Okay," I demanded, "what was that little scene all about? You might as well have told her I have some dreaded disease by the way she acted."

"I just wanted to see if she'd act jealous."

"Jealous of whom?"

She studied her fingertips. "You."

"Me? Why?"

"Cause she's had her eye on Tally since grade school. Her knowing you are there practically sitting in his lap all day'll keep her on her toes."

"I'm surprised at you. That was downright catty."

"I can't help myself."

"Well, she needn't worry. I'm totally burnt out on the male sex at this moment."

She cocked her head in question, so I told her the barest details about my shattered romance with Grant Jamerson, glossing over most of the painful details. "It was for the best, however. He'd have made a lousy husband."

As the noisy lunch crowd filled the room, I watched Lucinda and another waitress scurry from table to table. Five minutes later, she set the plates down in front of us without a word and managed the barest of smiles before rushing away.

I shook my head sadly. "Shame on you, Ginger. I've only been here nine days, and already I have a mortal enemy."

"Oh, flapdoodle. She'd have found out about you eventually any hoot. She keeps pretty close tabs on him."

I dug into my tuna salad. "So, they're an item?"

"If Tally was willing, she'd drag him to the preacher tomorrow. He's quite a catch y'know."

Ignoring her implication, I buttered a roll and yawned my disinterest. "To each his own, I guess."

"A gal could do worse."

I stopped eating. "Forget it, Ginger. I don't mean to sound condescending, but I can do better than a hired ranch hand."

She choked on her sandwich. "Ranch hand! Didn't anybody tell you? He and his family own the Starfire. It's one of the biggest dang cattle ranches in the state."

I felt like my chin was going to hit the table. The sparkle in Ginger's eyes reflected her enjoyment.

"Well, what's he doing working at that two bit...I mean at the paper?"

"He ain't been there but two years. He needed to get his mind off of what happened, I guess." A dreamy look came over her face. "It musta almost stopped his heart when he laid eyes on you the first time."

"Why?"

"With all that flaming red hair? He's gotta be thinking of his wife, Stephanie."

I'm sure my face looked incredulous. "If he's married, why should Lucinda be jealous of me?"

"He ain't married no more. Stephanie's dead as a doornail. Rode out one stormy night on one of them prize appaloosa horses of his and got throwed off. Died of a broken neck, she did." It was obvious by the satisfied gleam in her eyes that she was relishing every word.

"No kidding?"

"Yep. But that ain't the half of it." She lowered her voice. "Now, I ain't one for carryin' tales, but some folks 'round here didn't think it was an accident, including our very own John Dexter."

"Really? And, what did he think?"

"That Tally killed her."

Chapter Four

Ginger's remark blew me away. While the disclosure about Bradley was shocking, more intriguing yet was John Dexter's connection.

"Okay, you've got my undivided attention. Why did he suspect Bradley had anything to do with her death?"

She opened her mouth to speak when a loud voice from across the room cut her off. I turned to see Lucinda blocking the exit of a rather disheveled looking teen-ager clad in ragged jeans and tank top.

"This ain't a charity dining room. I'm sick to death of you free loaders jumping off the bus and coming in here to order up a meal you can't pay for!" She hustled the girl out the door. "You want a free meal, get your butt to the shelter three blocks over."

The teen cast a spiteful glance at Lucinda before slinking away, and I couldn't help but think of the young girl I'd picked up last week.

For a few seconds, the room was bathed in silence, and then one grizzled customer drawled, "Aw, Lucy. Now what'd you go an' do that for? She looked real pitiful, like a starved pup. You're not gonna go broke sharin' a sandwich with the kid." That brought a hoot of laughter from the man's companions.

Lucinda fixed him with a formidable glare. "You mind your own business, Elwood. I wouldn't care if it was just once in a while, but this is getting real old. It seems like every ragamuffin runaway in the country makes a beeline for my place. I can't afford to feed all of them. Let that Phillips woman do her job." With that she dusted her hands together and marched behind the counter.

"Poor little things," Ginger sighed, her expression troubled. "My sister Bonnie was showing me a magazine article just last week. They're called throwaway kids." Her voice got lower, more confidential. "As young as eleven or twelve they're turning tricks for food and money. Ain't that just shameful?"

"Awful. What shelter is Lucinda talking about?"

In between bites of her sandwich, she told me about the Desert Harbor Shelter located in a "big ol'" house on Tumbleweed, and run by a woman named Claudia Phillips. "I heard tell the place operates on a shoestring. She can't do a whole lot but give the kids some food and clothes and a place to stay a spell." Her tone turning ominous, she added, "Them are the lucky ones. Some of 'em just plain vanish."

"Vanish?"

"White slave traders."

"What are you talking about?"

"It was in all the papers. This gang was kidnapping blue-eyed blonde gals and selling 'em to them people over in the Middle East for their harems or some such thing."

"Oh, Ginger, get real."

"I swear on my mama's Bible! And then there was that bunch in Mexico snatching 'em up for human sacrifices."

Impatient to return to the previous subject, I steered the conversation back to John Dexter's suspicions about Bradley.

"Oh, yeah. Well, as I was sayin'..." She glanced at her watch and wailed, "Good Lord, it's almost one o'clock. Tugg's gonna have my fanny in a crack if I'm late again! I gotta scoot."

Twice now in two hours I'd let myself get sidetracked. "Wait a minute! You can't just drop a bombshell like that and then leave me hanging."

"Sorry, sugar. Lookee here. Why don't you come on over to supper tomorrow night? I'll rustle up a pot of my famous Texas chili, some homemade cornbread and fill in the rest."

"Okay."

She scribbled her address on a napkin and bolted out the door.

Aware that I had twenty minutes to kill before covering another terminally boring meeting at City Hall, I stepped outside, squinting into the glaring sunlight. I'd walked only a few feet from the door when one of Ginger's remarks struck me. Had I been so busy concentrating on what John Dexter had to do with Bradley's wife that I'd missed something important? Plopping down on the nearby shaded bus bench I pulled out the note Tugg had given me and read it again, zeroing in on the phrase, "dead teens."

I flipped open my notepad. In the center of the page, I drew a circle, wrote John Dexter's name in the middle, and then extended lines outward like bicycle spokes. On each line I placed one of the statements in the note, then leaned back against the hard wooden backrest to study it, only vaguely aware of people and traffic.

Was I way off base or could there be some connection between the dead teens and the runaways Ginger spoke of? Dexter had referred to something odd in some files at the sheriff's office. Were they the same ones he'd mentioned in the note?

I blew out a long breath. Obviously, I had my work cut out for me. On a new page, I made a note to go through past issues of the Sun and study the stories Dexter had written on the two cases. Step two would be the doozy; tactfully asking to see the files without agitating Roy Hollingsworth whom I'd finally met for the first time the previous Friday. Tugg had assigned me to cover the police blotter, or log as they called it. That would put me in the sheriff's office at least once a week.

I'd been surprised when I met Roy. From Tugg's description, I had expected to encounter a thoroughly uncooperative, disagreeable, perhaps even dangerous man. He appeared to be none of those, greeting me with a wide smile and a neighborly handshake. Standing well over six feet tall, his substantial stomach protruding over a gigantic turquoise belt buckle, he looked less like an adversary than he did a big, friendly bear. In uniform.

As we chatted, I couldn't help but stare at his curious eyebrows. They were light blonde, very fuzzy, and perched over his silver blue eyes like two giant caterpillars. I hid my surprise when he brought up the subject of John Dexter.

"Morty's been real unhappy with me over our manhunt for John Dexter, but as I tried to tell him, we can't produce the man out of thin air. Me and Deputy Potts, along with members of the sheriff's posse and other law enforcement agencies, combed this area for weeks and couldn't find a trace of him." Shrugging his aggravation, he added, "It's been real frustrating for me, too."

He was very convincing. I began to wonder if Tugg was on the wrong track. "I'm sure we'll hear from him sooner or later. When did you last see him?"

"Julie," he shouted. "Pull the file on John Dexter for me." Moments later, a slender, dark-haired girl appeared from another room and handed him a folder. The sheriff rifled through it as Julie and I exchanged introductions.

"He disappeared on March 29th, and I may have been the last person in town to see him. The reason I know that is because I wrote him a speeding ticket that day."

Tugg hadn't told me that. "Where did you ticket him?"

"Heading south on 89 toward Phoenix. He seemed real nervous when I stopped him. Agitated. He was...well, let's say, verbally abusive, but for John that wasn't out of character." He smiled wryly. "So you see, I don't think anything unusual happened to John. I think he had something else going. Why he didn't give Morty notice, I don't know." When he frowned, the two blond caterpillars fused together into one.

While he shuffled papers into the file, I decided either he was being quite up front with me or he was a remarkably good actor. He'd ushered me to the door, inviting me to come anytime or call him if I had any questions. Because he'd been so damned likable, it would make my job all the harder.

A screech of brakes jolted me back to the present. I closed the notepad and rose stiffly from the bus bench. The meeting ran for over two hours, and it was late afternoon when I returned to the newspaper office. Ginger greeted me with a smile reminding me again of dinner the following evening. I hauled out three boxes of back issues of the paper to take home with me.

The wind was blowing across the desert floor, whipping up funnels of yellow dust when I reached the house. Before going inside, I paused as I always did to admire the spectacle of Castle Rock. Ever changeable, depending on the angle of the sun, it glowed in shades of peach and burnished copper.

After an early dinner, I phoned my parents. They seemed pleased I was settling in. Dad asked about my job, Morton Tuggs, and my asthma. With forced enthusiasm, I told them about my new life and promised to call them again soon. As I hung up the phone, a sharp pang of homesickness enveloped me. To ward off the blues, I turned up the television and cleaned the kitchen.

Still filled with restless energy, I went outside to sweep the walkway and water the small front garden filled with a bright yellow sea of desert daisies. The sound of a vehicle made me look up. The black Mercedes I'd seen the first day purred down Lost Canyon Road followed by a white van. Was that perhaps my nearest neighbor, Dr. Price? I'd been meaning to check out Serenity House for days now, but hadn't had the time. I decided a nice long walk would do me good. Mary Tuggs had said it was about two miles away, so I should be back before dark.

It was so quiet I could hear my tennis shoes crunching on the rocky road. Except for the birds and an occasional gust of wind, nothing disturbed the silence.

When I reached a fork in the road, I chose the left which looked well traveled. The right fork, overgrown with tall grass and tumbleweeds, snaked off into the desert. I slowed my footsteps as I approached a large sign with bold red letters announcing: DANGER! NO UNAUTHORIZED PERSONNEL BEYOND THIS POINT.

The high fence topped with jagged coils of razor wire looked ominous, but in a way it made me feel secure to know it was there. For a fleeting second, visions of violent ax-wielding mental patients flashed through my mind like scenes from a cheap horror movie. "Don't be stupid," I muttered under my breath. I'd read that many of the new drugs did an excellent job of subduing patients.

I peered through the chain-link fence. Enclosed inside a second fence I spotted the top of an ancient bell tower. Patches of red tile roofs and white stucco buildings were visible among the groves of palms and cottonwood trees. It looked quite peaceful and not at all threatening.

Then, seemingly from out of nowhere, two enormous Dobermans rushed to the fence, eyes gleaming, teeth snapping, their throaty barks echoing through the stillness. Whoa! I jumped back, heart pounding. Without hesitation, I retreated. All during the walk home, the memory of the dogs' snarling faces kept me in a state of watchful anxiety.

Sometime during the night, the wind kicked up again. It whistled around under the eaves and rattled the windows. For hours, I thrashed about restlessly. When I finally did fall into a deep sleep I kept having the same annoying dream over and over. A voice kept calling for me to get out. "Get out. Get out."

The persistent phrase was so irritating, I finally opened my eyes. Then I heard it again. Was I awake or still dreaming?

"Get out!" The voice was quite distinct that time. This was no dream! Pulse racing, I sat bolt upright in bed and stared at the partially open patio door. "Who's out there?"

Besides the murmur of the wind rustling through the trees, I thought I heard footsteps disappearing into the distance.